COMMITTED

COMMITTED

THE ASCENSION MYTH™ BOOK 9

ELL LEIGH CLARKE

MICHAEL ANDERLE

COMMITTED TEAM

JIT Beta Readers

Daniel Weigert
Trista McIntire
Tim Bischoff
John Ashmore
Kim Boyer
Veronica Torres
Joshua Ahles
Paul Westman
Edward Rosenfeld
Micky Cocker
Larry Omans

If we missed anyone, please let us know!

Editor
Eric Martinez

To everyone who ever dreamed of making a dent in the universe.

— Ellie

To Family, Friends and
Those Who Love
To Read.
May We All Enjoy Grace
To Live The Life We Are
Called.

— Michael

CHAPTER ONE

Aboard <u>*The Scamp Princess*, Kirox Quadrant</u>

"Okay, space cowboy, you're up!" Scamp announced cockily over the cockpit audio.

Sean opened one eye and then the other, his dream of naked ladies catering to his every whim while he fired guns on the test range evaporating away to reveal his harsh reality.

He eased himself into an upright position in his console chair and turned up the heat in the cold cockpit. "Thank you, Scamp," he mumbled as gracefully as he could manage. He started poking at the holoscreen keys, checking and double-checking before setting a scan.

"Sean?"

"Yes, Scamp?"

"Why are we checking for short range transmissions?"

"Because we're trying to pick up a short-wave, short-range transmission at these precise coordinates."

"Oh."

Silence fell over the cockpit for a few moments, before:

"Sean?"

"Yes, Scamp?"

"Why?"

Sean finished what he was doing and then sat back in his self-adjusting console chair. "Because this is what Karina and I agreed. We'd leave a short-range beacon right here at this location, with the location of our actual meeting point."

"Why, though?"

"Because even if someone somehow knew about these coordinates, they would never know to look for a tiny beacon that wouldn't show up more than a kilometer from here."

Scamp paused for a moment, processing. "Oh. Right. That's smart."

"Yes. It is."

Beep beep beep. A light on the pilot's screen started flashing urgently.

"Looks like we've found your beacon, then," Scamp commented.

"Looks like it." Sean watched, waiting for the signal to settle and then ran it through a descrambling program he'd uploaded from his holo before his power nap.

"Okay, Scamp, those are our next coordinates. Shoot out the beacon with the auxiliary lasers, and then let's get going."

"Are you sure you want to do that?"

"What do you mean?"

"Well, if anyone needs to track you—"

"This is the point. I don't want anyone tracking me. It's not safe. Blow it up, and then let's get going. She's in trouble."

Obediently and without any further comment, Scamp locked on to the signal. "Armed and ready on your command, sir."

"Fire!" Sean commanded.

Pew. A laser shot out from the undercarriage of *The Scamp Princess.*

Pop.

Sean shoved his bottom lip out and shifted sheepishly in his chair. "Well, that was anticlimatic."

"I'm sure you've heard that a lot."

"Ha, you're hilarious, Scamp," he retorted dryly to his EI.

Scamp sniggered at his own joke. "I guess it was just a tiny beacon, after all."

Sean glanced at Scamp's screen, raising one eyebrow, knowing full well Scamp couldn't see him. "Indeed. Okay, Scamp, let's go."

One moment, the ship was there, hanging in the blackness. A second later, it had popped out of existence, leaving barely a ripple of a particle trail as it gated to its next destination.

Calzone Offices, Bronislovas Trading Outpost, Kirox Quadrant

Vito Calzone stood at the window of his office, watching the ships coming and going from the dock just across the way. The colored lights blipped and ambled before coming to a halt in the dock or disappearing in a flash as they tripped into sub-light and tripped out of the system in the blink of an eye.

The door of his office swished open quietly. Calzone didn't turn around. He didn't need to. "You know," he mused philosophically, "they're like fireflies."

An anxious voice replied, "Sir?"

"These spaceships," Vito drawled in an old accent from the region going several generations back. "They never existed like this when I was a kid. And now, they're in and out of here like fireflies. One blip and they're gone again."

"Yes, sir."

Calzone kept watching them, still not turning around to look at his visitor.

"Okay, Roberto. What's so important?"

"Sir, it's… well. We've noticed money coming into one of your guys' accounts."

"That's not unusual."

"No, sir. But it's not from us."

Calzone turned around and took a few steps to his desk chair. "And who do we think it was from?"

There was a slight pause before Roberto answered. "The sender is Ms. Karina Duffy."

Calzone waved his hands. "That supposed to mean something to me?"

"Well, erm, if you remember, she was one of her favorite assassins."

"So what? You're saying someone is sending us a message?"

"Possibly, sir. Unless…"

"Unless what?"

"Unless she's still alive."

"She's not alive," Vito snapped. "And even if she were, she's dead to me. Whose account is it?"

"Ronnie's, sir."

"Who?"

"Ronnie Matherson. He works on Bill's side of the family."

Calzone nodded wisely, as if he remembered. He took his time and sat down at his desk. "So," he said slowly, "looks like someone is paying Ronnie money."

Roberto nodded, then swallowed hard. "Unless that's what they want us to think, of course," he added. There was an awkward pause. "Sir, what would you like me to do?"

Calzone lowered his eyes in contemplation. "I'll handle it," he said quietly. "Keep an eye out for anything else, though."

"Yes, sir."

"Send in Churchill."

"Yes, sir."

The lanky computer ops nerd headed back across the carpeted office and hit the close button for the door on the panel behind him as he left.

Moments later, the door whooshed gently open again.

"You wanted to see me, sir?" Churchill was broad and stocky.

He ran a team on the west side and reported in directly to the Don. Thirty years of service, and he never once took a day off. Nor did he have any trouble from within the ranks of the family.

Calzone regarded the loyal soldier carefully as he approached his desk. "We have reason to suspect Ronnie is going outside of the family."

"You want me to take care of him?"

"No. I want you to follow him and find out what he's up to and who he's up to it with."

"No problem, boss. I can have someone on it immediately."

"No," the Don said firmly. "Do it yourself. And this stays between us."

Churchill lowered his head in deference. "Yes, sir. Of course, sir."

"That's all," Vito said, dismissing him.

Churchill backed up a few steps before turning and hurrying out again.

The Don leaned back in his leather covered anti-grav chair, steepling his fingers in front of him.

Base restrooms, Gaitune-67

Molly couldn't stop her eyes from streaming. Her hands over her mouth, she tried to stifle the sobs. She leaned back against the wall of the restroom stall and put her hands to her head. It was throbbing.

It's okay. We're going to find him.

You can't know that. What does the evidence say?

Molly sobbed again, thankful that she could have this conversation in her head and not have to speak the words. That would make it too real.

We don't have enough data to conclude that he's dead. And until we have the data pulled from Scamp, we won't have a

clue about what happened. Be patient. Don't write him off so soon. Scamp only returned twenty minutes ago.

Molly didn't respond. Her mind just couldn't engage in conversation. She could barely see through her eyes, she had cried so hard.

I have to go. They're waiting.

You've got a few more minutes. They'll understand. They're processing for themselves, too. They've never seen a ship return without a crew, either.

You mean they're also crying.

No. But they're worried and trying to wrap their heads around what might have happened.

They're all in the conference room?

Yes. Mostly.

Okay. I've got to move.

Molly wiped her face with her hands and grabbed some tissue to dry them. She fumbled with the lock on the door and headed out to the basins. She hardly dared look at herself in the mirror. There was no way she would be able to fix the swollen eyes before walking in to face her team and give them their orders.

She opened the faucet and watched the water for a moment. Then she looked up.

Fuck.

It's not that bad.

Not that bad? What do you know? You're an AI.

I've been monitoring your body the whole time we've been connected. With cold water, you can reduce the swelling to acceptable levels. I'd suggest dabbing with a wet towel, though.

If she hadn't been so distraught, she might have smiled at the notion of her AI giving her tactical beauty advice. She splashed water on her face and looked at herself again, pulling a blonde strand back from her face and hooking it behind her ear.

That's going to have to do.

Well then, your subjects await.

Molly grabbed a paper towel and dried her face and hands before dropping the towel in the trash and heading out.

Turning left out of the corridor, she strode confidently up to the conference room and walked straight in. She did a quick assessment of who was present.

"Where's Brock?" she asked.

Crash answered. "He's already working on Scamp. He's pulling every scrap of data to find out where he was and what happened."

"Okay." She closed the door and strode around to the head of the table. She didn't sit though. "Here's the plan. As soon as we have the coordinates, we're going after Sean."

She turned to Crash, who was sitting bolt upright awaiting instructions. "Crash, help Brock. Do whatever he needs to get us that data and get us airborne in The Empress."

Molly turned to look at Joel and Jack on the left-hand side of the table. "You two are on supplies. Which includes weapons. Lots of them."

Joel almost smiled. If the situation hadn't been so tense, Molly suspected briefly that he would have punched the air.

Boys and guns, she thought, mentally rolling her eyes.

"Pieter and Oz," she continued swiftly. "Start working on the data as Brock pulls it. Paige, you're running point for this investigation. Let the general know Scamp is back, and see if there is anything else the Federation can tell us based on the data Pieter gathers."

Paige raised her hand and spoke fast. "What about telling Giles and Arlene?"

Molly paused only long enough to draw breath. "Oz will take care of that. Maya you're on food supplies. But, then I need you and Paige to work from here when we leave. Any questions?"

Pieter raised his hand awkwardly. "What about Bourne?"

Molly's brow furrowed. "What's he doing?"

"Still binge-watching the archives," Pieter said judgmentally.

Molly thought for a moment. "Is he likely to do anything else until we get back?"

Oz's voice connected over the intercom for the conference room. "Unlikely, if past behavior is an indicator of future."

"Fine," Molly concluded. "Let's leave him be. Anything else?" Molly's gaze flicked around the room.

Everyone was silent. They knew what they had to do.

"Okay. Wheels up in two hours. Dismissed."

No one spoke as they pushed back on the anti-grav chairs and filed hurriedly out of the conference room. Molly stayed out of their way for a minute while they vacated.

What do you want to tell Giles and Arlene?

That Scamp came back, and we're going after his last known location. But Giles isn't coming. He needs to stay here and look after things at the University.

And when he argues?

Tell him I'm putting my foot down.

Okay. On it.

Thanks, Oz.

Molly followed her team out of the doors and into the base corridors. She also had work to do before they left, and two hours was almost no time to get her head in gear.

<u>Bates Residence, Estaria</u>

The house was quiet. Philip knew it would be hours before Carol got home. Even on a regular week, she'd be the last one in the office. But he knew from her patterns and mood that this had been no regular week.

Their operative code kept them from discussing agency business at home. Carol insisted it was better for their relationship anyway. Philip wasn't convinced. But that was what he had signed up for during his exit interview, knowing full well his wife would remain inside the fold when he stepped out.

No disclosure and therefore no lies, he reminded himself.

He paused, knowing full well what it would mean if he was discovered. Part of him didn't care. Part of him was more concerned about protecting his daughter. He'd replayed the conversation he and Carol had had in the parking lot that day after seeing Molly... and Sean. No way had his wife really let it go, despite her protests that she had nearly been rumbled and had learned her lesson.

Carol didn't learn lessons.

She just adapted.

He glanced over at the window for one final check. It was still daylight. And no sign of her car.

He sat down at the family terminal. Though the EI had been stripped out a long time ago, well before they'd moved to this property, certain things did remain. Like the agency-grade firewall and military-grade defense arrays. They weren't stupid. They needed to protect their XtraNET connection. Plus, there were certain things they needed access to at all times, especially now that Carol was the head of the agency.

He woke the holoscreen and started picking his way through the security protocols. Technically, he wouldn't have clearance. But he knew his wife well, and guessing her passwords had historically been a breeze.

The grandfather clock ticked pointedly in the hallway, pretending as though everything was just as peaceful as usual. But the hint of the seconds going past niggled in the back of Philip's mind. He took a deep breath and entered the last protocol.

ACCESS GRANTED.

Yes! Still got it! He smiled to himself.

He ferreted through the most likely files. Anything under something inane like "Archive" was a likely candidate. He quickly found old case files mixed in with current ops. Most of them didn't interest him. Just the usual stuff he used to deal with as an operative: politicians, unusual trading activity, statistically anomalous spikes in data or energy in core threat areas…

None of it was what he needed.

He kept rummaging, opening files methodically and eyeballing them as fast as he could.

Then he found a text file. It was labeled "Notes". His brain honed in. The file contained a couple of strings of numbers. They looked like the right kind of length for them to be access codes for a network tap.

Gotcha!

He quickly memorized the strings. If these were what he thought they were, they would allow him to tap into whatever the live string was on the network that connected directly up to the target. He'd have to be careful. Her techs would be able to see him access it, and the action would be time stamped, too. There would be logs. Detailed logs. But it would potentially give him the last bit of proof he needed when he finally found out what she was up to.

He started to close the holoscreens down, but then something caught his eye.

He stopped.

There was a link to her internal calendar. He poked it, and it opened up on another screen. He took a quick look, two weeks back and two weeks forward, mentally checking that against what he knew of her movements. She'd been late a number of times this week. Last night, she'd said she had a department meeting. But there was nothing in the calendar. Otherwise, it was convincingly populated.

He closed his eyes, checking he'd memorized it all correctly, then closed the holo. Shutting down the terminal, he wandered back to the kitchen, gathering his thoughts.

Snack and then thinking time, he told himself.

Several hours later, the Sark had gone down.

Dinner time had come and gone.

All that remained was a dish that was ready to be relegated to the fridge for when Carol returned.

Philip sat reading in his favorite armchair in the living room when he heard the car pull up in the driveway.

There was the familiar clatter at the door and then in the hallway as Carol made her way inside.

"You're pretty damn noisy for a spook!" her husband called playfully.

Her heels clipped across the floor and into the living space. She brought the scent of the night air in with her. "Well, it's a good thing I wasn't sneaking around then," she retorted.

She appeared in the doorway, looking just as exhausted as every other day for weeks.

Philip smiled. "What've you been up to?"

She unceremoniously plonked her purse down on the chair by the door. "Just working late."

"On what?"

Carol paused. "You know I can't answer that." She looked at him quizzically.

Philip got up, still smiling, and walked into the open-plan kitchen. "You know I know better than to just let it go." He picked up the bottle of wine and reached for a couple of glasses, which he placed gently on the counter.

Carol approached the counter, drawn in by the idea of the alcohol hitting her system. "Yes, your tenacity is one of the reasons I married you. It's late." She looked around the kitchen for clues. "Have you eaten?"

"Yes, but I saved you some. How about I heat it up and pour you a glass," he poured the wine, "and you can tell me all about your day?"

Carol eyed him suspiciously. She had been married to a spy

for nearly thirty years. "Sounds good. Let me just go and get out of this atmosuit, and then we can relax."

She wandered out, feeling his gaze on her back.

Dinner passed with very little probing. Carol wondered if maybe Philip realized that he was breaching protocol and had decided to back off.

Or maybe he just forgot that he had been suspicious? She smiled to herself as she gently drifted off to sleep in the soft bedclothes and half-light from the city beyond the bedroom window.

Philip waited until her breathing had settled to a slower rate and then made his move.

Carefully and slowly, he slipped out from between the bed covers and padded around the room. He reached her bedside table and lifted her holo from the charging pad. It lit up, but he moved it so that the light wouldn't disturb his wife.

Slowly, he moved out into the hallway. The bathroom would normally have been a better option but too noisy. The dark quiet of the landing served him better.

He flicked straight through to the screens he needed. Flicking through the latest progress reports that had come in since she left the office.

From what he could make out, it was a Dark Net Op, or DNO. They had a whole team who handled this particular type of operation. The reports were stacked with probe responses and hypotheses. There weren't any real interpretations of what their data was telling them, but it seemed that perhaps they were trying to figure out the owners and users of certain Estarian-based servers, under massive encryption and cyber security protocols.

Nothing unusual in itself.

He breathed, trying to slow his thinking for clarity. He wasn't going to figure it all out tonight. But this was at least another piece of the puzzle. Maybe.

He closed the holoscreens and tapped the button to set them back to unread so they wouldn't be deleted off the server before she could see them. That would be a red flag if there was anything in there that the rest of the team referenced later.

And this was a long game.

As quietly as he could, he padded back into the bedroom and replaced the holo. Just as he was walking around to his side of the bed, he felt her stir. Instinctively, he headed straight for the bathroom door and then closed it a little more loudly than he would have otherwise.

She muttered something.

"Sorry," he whispered across the room to her. She rolled over, and he clambered back into bed next to her.

CHAPTER TWO

Aboard *The Scamp Princess*, Hangar Deck, Gaitune-67

"Okay, another twenty minutes, and that will be all of it. Oz, you got that?"

"Yes. Downloading fine."

"Good." Brock leaned back on his haunches from under the console of *The Scamp Princess*. He started tidying his tools away.

Crash rocked gently in the navigator's seat. "Sure there's nothing I can do?"

Brock unplugged a connector from the console he had a device hooked into. "Not yet. Not until we've got any clue about where we're going." He winked at Crash.

Crash leaned an arm on the nearest console. "Okay. Well as soon as we do, I can get the coordinates plugged in and find out what we'll be walking into."

Brock continued to clean up tools and pieces of debris he'd left strewn around as he worked. "Yeah. That's a good idea. Shit, I can't believe that all the time we were talking about our vacay, Sean was sitting there contemplating taking off without us."

Crash just watched Brock.

"Makes me feel guilty for having gone away," he continued.

"Hey, we needed a break," Crash said flatly. "And maybe if Sean took a day off once in a while, he wouldn't be wound so tightly."

Brock snorted at the thought of Sean heading out to Club Sark with them. "Yeah. You may have a point. You don't think he's actually… you know? I mean, Scamp wouldn't leave him if he were still alive so…" He left the thought hanging in the air, wanting closure, but also not wanting to be told his friend was dead.

Crash shook his head. "Stop thinking like that. He wouldn't be the first military tool to bite off more than he can chew. Don't worry. We'll find him and bring him home," he told him decisively. "And then give him shit about running off to save damsels on his own."

Brock sighed. "Yeah. You're right." He packed away the last of the tools, leaving one connector hooked up to the console. "Okay, I'm going to take this lot over to *The Empress*. Nothing we can do until Oz finishes that transfer."

Crash hauled himself to his feet. "Okay. I'll pack a bag. Want me to do one for you, too?"

Brock nodded and rested his hand on Crash's bicep as they headed out of the cockpit. "Thanks, man."

Crash patted him gently on the back, comforting him. "It's all gonna be fine," he reiterated.

The pair made their way through the passage to the side door and carefully headed down the invisible staircase to the hangar deck.

Aboard *The Empress*, Hangar Deck, Gaitune-67

The crew clambered on board *The Empress*. It was familiar territory and comforting, despite the unspoken dread that their mission may already be a failure before it had begun.

And yet, no one dared admit that Sean may already be dead.

Jack plonked herself opposite Pieter, who was more anxious than normal. She smiled at him reassuringly, without being too nice. Too friendly, and he would know that they were worried, and that would stop his brain from doing what they needed him to do.

She glanced over at Joel. Joel nodded, catching on to her tactic to keep Pieter calm.

Pieter, oblivious, threw his pack into an overhead locker and sat down. A moment later, he was up again and fussing with his pack. Jack watched without looking directly at him, smiling to herself as if she were just a fly on the wall. Detached. Collected.

Molly was the last one to board. Joel had seen her giving her instructions to Paige. He hovered, not quite deciding where he would sit. Jack was on to him. He was going to pull "Operation: Calm Molly Down."

She stomped through the cabin with her pack and gun belt thrown over her shoulder. Her holo hadn't been closed down, and if she had been wearing boots with laces, Joel guessed they wouldn't have been tied, either.

She threw her pack down on a lounge chair and collapsed next to it, preventing anyone from sitting next to her.

Joel, quick as a flash, grabbed his jacket and mirrored her move by throwing his jacket down in the chair opposite her and plonking himself down across from her.

That was as close as he was going to get. Clearly.

The gentle hum of the drive started up. Crash's normal banter was nowhere to be heard in the liftoff process. In fact, Molly found herself checking out the window to confirm they were indeed airborne and heading out of the hangar. Only Emma's voice recited the normal announcements and safety notices.

Molly closed her eyes and allowed the process to wash over her. She tried to still her mind as Arlene had taught her in her realm-jumping training.

Her body was a mishmash of emotions. Emotions she'd rather not have to deal with right now.

She felt a nudge on her leg and reluctantly opened one eye, letting the outside world invade. Joel was looking at her pointedly. He'd nudged his knee against hers.

"What?"

"Wondering if you're ready to talk." He nodded at her bag on the seat in front of him. She took the hint and moved it to the one opposite her where he'd dumped his jacket. Joel deftly moved from his seat to the one next to her and buckled his harness.

"You're taking this hard," he said quietly.

Molly shoved her arm onto the outside armrest and stared out of the window. Her other shoulder half shrugged.

"I know you don't want to talk about it," Joel persisted, "but we need to. *You* need to."

Molly turned her head and glared at him.

"I'm here for you," he continued, ignoring the glare and looking straight ahead of him now. He knew how to handle Molly and her avoidance strategies. She just needed to feel safe enough to open up.

And not pushed.

He readjusted himself in his chair so that his upper arm was touching hers. He felt her defenses come down. All the hardness that she used to shield herself from her own feelings melted, and a single tear trickled down her face.

She sniffed as quietly as she could and rummaged for a tissue to catch the tears before anyone else could see.

"I don't know how much longer I can keep doing this," she confided.

Joel's gaze snapped to her. She continued to look down at the tissue, avoiding his eyes. "What's changed?" he asked.

Molly shrugged. He could see the tension welling inside of her again. He didn't want her to start crying here in front of the crew. She wouldn't want that, and it wasn't fair to her. But she needed to process.

He leaned in a little more. "Is this about Sean?"

"Kinda. But also everything else." She paused and swiped away another tear. "It's just one thing after another. It feels like it never ends. I'm exhausted."

Joel bobbed his head and pressed his arm more against hers. She responded and leaned into him, resting her head on his shoulder. He glanced over at Jack and Pieter, wondering if he should put his arm around her, or whether that would arouse too much interest from the others.

He decided against it. "Hey. It's okay. We're going to get through this."

"Will we?" she asked combatively. "I just can't help thinking that if I wasn't around, none of this would be happening."

Joel frowned. "What are you talking about?"

"Sean. He wouldn't have needed to go off on his own. He'd still be with the Federation and have their backup."

Joel's brow furrowed deeper, confused at what she was saying.

Molly continued. "You can't ignore the fact that his relationship with them has become strained because of his relationship with us."

Joel hesitated, processing what she was saying. "Well, there may be some truth to that, but that's not going to get him killed. And it's certainly not your fault. What's really going on?"

Molly pursed her lips. "Sean came to see me before he disappeared."

"About his mission?"

"No. About *me*."

"What do you mean?"

"He thinks I have some ability to push my will onto people. Another side effect. He was going to report it to Lance, and I asked him not to."

"And now he's gone, and you're feeling guilty."

Molly sniffed, finally finding the strength to bring her gaze up to meet Joel's. "And wondering if somehow I also influenced him to disappear…"

Joel put his arm around her. "That's just crazy talk. I mean, even if you could push your will onto other people, you would never want him dead. You're just not wired that way."

"But what if it was a component of his decision making?"

Joel shook his head. "No way," he told her firmly. "This thought process is a pattern you run. You look for ways to make things your fault. Or your responsibility."

Molly allowed herself to sink against his body, allowing his arm around her to stay. "How do you figure that?" she mumbled.

"Look at all the things that have happened: the way you want to change every injustice on Estaria. The way you relate to each team member personally, helping them to find their groove. No way you could even accidentally do what you're suggesting."

Molly pulled away and tried to look at Joel. "You think I'm doing things wrong?"

"No," he corrected her. "I think there is a reason that you're wired this way, and if we understood it better, you wouldn't need to feel so damn guilty all the time. So, what is it?"

"What do you mean?"

"Well, what happened in your childhood? What is this really about?"

Molly thought for a long while, even though her mind had jumped immediately to what the issue was that Joel was trying to get out of her.

Eventually she spoke, sitting up a little. Joel removed his arm.

"I was about twelve. I'd been hacking into my parent's EI to find out stuff. Actually, stuff about *The Empress*. Rumors. History. Missions. There wasn't much, but I used the EI because it had greater reach, beyond just the local Estarian network."

Joel nodded.

"Well," she continued, "my parents had told me it was off

limits. Turns out, they had been using it for the business and had taken it offline because they were attracting heat from certain criminal elements in their line of work."

"And you got it back online?"

She nodded, fiddling with her tissue. "Yeah. I must have triggered some flags or something because one night, I heard something in the house. And shouting. I went downstairs and there were men in the house—in full combat gear. With guns."

"Who were they?"

Molly shook her head. "I dunno. Dark ops. Mercenaries. We never found out. But they took my parents. At gun point."

"Philip and Carol?"

She nodded again.

"But they're still alive," Joel reminded her, trying to understand what had happened.

"Yeah," she agreed. "No thanks to me. They managed to escape somehow. Goodness knows how. They said something about having some help. They were gone for about a day. It was the worst day of my life. The police kept asking me questions about what happened, and their work, and their business. I didn't know anything, but they treated me like a criminal. Like I knew what was happening.

"After they came back, the police had very few questions, and everything just seemed to go back to normal again. They wrapped up that business a few years later when Dad retired and Mom got some kind of government job. And we never really talked about it again. They just said it wasn't my fault and that they were fine, so it didn't matter."

Joel frowned.

"But it was my fault," she insisted. "If I hadn't been poking around with that EI, none of it would have happened."

Her voice started to break. Joel put his arm around her again as she sobbed quietly.

"Look," he whispered. "I know it feels like it's your fault, but things happen. Maybe the EI wasn't the trigger. Maybe it was. They should have told you why the EI was offline. And besides, they're still alive and doing fine. Something tells me that whatever they went through, it can't have been that bad."

Molly's face was hidden from him. He felt his T-shirt getting wet from her tears. He held her tighter and continued to whisper in her ear. "It wasn't your fault. You were a kid. You didn't have all the information... and you don't know what other good things that served."

Her muffled voice spoke into his T-shirt. "I don't understand..."

"Well, think about it. Maybe it was the shock your folks needed to get out of that business they were in. Sometimes these things demand too much of us, either in terms of risks we need to take or in terms of working too hard. Sounds like your folks were already taking risks, for those kinds of people to show up at the house."

Molly's sobbing subsided, and she became still.

"Also," Joel continued, "imagine if they'd continued, and your dad didn't retire. Maybe he would have ended up working too hard and giving himself a heart attack or something. Maybe your mum would have had problems if she hadn't taken a more low-pressure job in the government."

Molly nodded her head, still up against Joel's T-shirt.

He squeezed her reassuringly under his arm. "Sounds like that was a well-timed warning shot to me. And they don't seem too traumatized by any of it."

She sat up. "No. You're right. They were fine afterward. But that was the unnerving thing. Everything went back to business as usual."

Joel's eyes flickered with some kind of recognition.

"What?" Molly pressed.

Joel took a deep breath, thinking. "Well, I wonder... have you talked to them about it since? You know, now that you're grown up and all?"

Molly shook her head. "I've barely spoken to them at all since I escaped to university early."

Joel pursed his lips. "Well, our perceptions as kids are super different from the reality of what happened. Sometimes, we misinterpret things, or we misunderstand. We try and make sense of it from the schemas that we're operating from at the time, but as we get older, we have more understanding of the world. You know, you're a lot older now. And you've seen a huge amount. You've got all your life and military experience. You think maybe if you talked to them about it now, you might understand it better?"

Molly sat herself up again, drying her eyes. "Yeah, probably," she admitted.

Joel smiled. "Of course, it would mean braving your parents again. But it would probably be worth it." He paused. "I'd come with you if that would help?"

Molly hesitated.

"No pressure," he added. "I'm here for you, though."

She bobbed her head then lunged forward to her bag on the other seat, rummaging for another tissue as a distraction. "Yeah, maybe. When we get Sean back…"

Joel put a hand on her back and rubbed it soothingly. "Okay, when we've got Sean back," he agreed.

He checked over his shoulder, briefly catching Jack's eye. Jack looked away quickly, respectful of their semi-privacy. Pieter looked like he had his implant feeding him sound and was off in his own little world.

Joel kicked back his seat and pretended to relax. He knew it was good for Molly for him to just hang nearby. Even if she didn't understand that herself right now.

· · ·

Aboard *The Empress*

Joel, Jack, and Pieter sat quietly, spread out through the main cabin of *The Empress*. Pieter had several holoscreens open and seemed to be continuing the work he had started as soon as they had access to Scamp's data.

Molly gazed out of the window, her thoughts dancing from sensations of anxiety, to sadness, to determination, and back again.

"Molly?" Crash interrupted her thoughts through her audio implant.

Molly hit her audio device. "'Sup?"

"We've got a call coming in via the ship's quiet link. It's Giles, calling from *The Scamp Princess*."

"Okay, patch him through." She sat up in her seat and took a deep breath.

"Hi, Molly." Giles's voice announced himself in her ear. He sounded uncomfortable.

"Giles, hi. Everything okay?"

"Well, yes. Although not really. I heard about Sean, of course."

Molly leaned her head backwards against her headrest, her gaze flicking to the ceiling. "Yes, we're on our way to his last known location now."

"Good. Oz told you I offered my services?"

Molly assumed that was a question, even though his intonation suggested otherwise. "He did. Thank you."

"Okay. Well, erm, the other thing is, we've had a lead on the talisman thing. So, erm… if you've cleared Scamp for duty, would you mind if Arlene and I went and chased this lead down?"

Molly processed the request for a moment. Her mind scrambled for any reasons for or against. Anything that wasn't insurmountable. Then she hit one.

"What about the part where I needed you at the university to make sure everything is handled there?"

"Oh… erm. Right. Of course."

There was a silence on the line. Molly felt Joel looking over at her but chose to remain focused on one conversation at a time. She knew he'd only interject in favor of Giles.

She spoke again. "How long do you think it will take?"

"Well, you know how these things are…"

"I have an idea," she said.

"What if I promise to be back before the semester starts up again?"

"Yes, that would be fine. But stay in touch with Paige, and make sure that she can make any decisions that need making for the school."

"Right you are. Thanks Molly. And… good luck."

"You too, Giles. Good hunting."

She could hear him breathing on the line for a second or two longer. She wondered if he might have something else to say. And then the line went dead. She turned her head and gazed out the window, watching the stars shift around them. She didn't have the brain power to allocate any to Professor Kurns right now. She needed to stay laser focused on finding Sean.

CHAPTER THREE

Philip sat peacefully on the patio, reading a spy thriller.

Wrong, wrong, wrong, he tutted, swiping to the next page on his holo.

Just then, his wrist buzzed, alerting him to an incoming call. He accepted it, seeing who it was. "Hi, Tray, how are you?" he asked brightly.

"Hi, Philip. Good. All good. It's a work call."

"Okay, go ahead," Philip responded in a more muted tone.

"Well, you asked for me to give you a heads up if there was anything unusual going on around the Royale asset?"

"Yes. You got something?"

"Yeah, seems he's gone off grid," Tray said.

"On a mission?"

"Probably. Knowing him."

"Anything happening with the Federation?" Philip asked.

"That's above my clearance."

"Ah, yes. Of course. But if you hear anything…"

"You'll be the first to know."

"Okay thanks, Tray."

"No problem," Tray responded. "See you on the course next week."

"Yes, see you then," Philip said brightly again. He closed the holo call and sat in silence for a few seconds before pulling up a new screen.

He typed the command.

>> Connect FED.

>> Return.

A new screen appeared. This one was slightly red in tone and had nothing but a black screen and a flashing cursor.

He typed the following:

>>   ArchAngel://Agent   5673#delta.   Suspected   978 infringement.

>> Is Royale on a dark op for you folks?

He waited, watching the flashing cursor. He hated this bit. He rarely used the interface for obvious reasons, but every time he had reason to, it had been because there was an imminent threat to planetary security, and ArchAngel was a known ally who would occasionally intervene.

This wasn't exactly a planetary matter. Although, if his suspicions were right, it would certainly be something the Federation would want to be involved in.

He hated the waiting, though.

He tried to relax and enjoy the fresh air and the sun starting to go down, but his eyes were compulsively drawn back to the red-hued screen and the damn flashing cursor.

He sighed, watching the flashing.

Finally, something happened.

>>> What is the nature of the infringement?

Philip considered how he might type the explanation and then resigned himself to the reality that to speak it would be more efficient.

>> Can we speak?

A link appeared. Philip clicked it and felt his audio implant connect into the new protocol.

"Hello?" he asked quietly.

"Hello, Philip. What is the nature of the infringement?"

"Well, it's not exactly that. But it *is* rather sensitive."

"How so?" ArchAngel's computer-generated voice spoke into his audio implant.

"Well, it's my wife. She's been tracking Molly, I think, and I wanted to know why. And we saw that Royale was in cahoots with her, so I had a buddy of mine let me know if anything strange happened around Royale, rather than trying to interfere. Anyway, he's just let me know that Sean went dark last week. No one's seen or heard from him since. I wondered if you had him on a mission."

There was a slight pause before ArchAngel responded. "No, we don't. Let me try and find him."

There was a longer pause before ArchAngel spoke again. "I can't get a read on him. Turns out the team he was posted with hasn't seen him. They're on a mission to find him right now."

"You mean *Molly's* team?"

"That's correct."

"What can you tell me?" Philip's voice cracked with anxiety, wondering if his actions had put Molly in danger.

"They're retracing his steps. I've pulled news footage from the area. Processing now." Another pause. "Okay. We have a hit. Sean seems to have been kidnapped from a trading outpost. Along with a girl."

"Molly?"

"No, Molly is with her team on *The Empress*."

"Is she in danger?"

"She does a dangerous job. But imminently? Not that we know of. Hang on."

The line cracked and then went quiet, as if there was a low white-noise feed being broadcast.

ArchAngel returned to the call. "It seems your wife has been probing the servers that Molly and her team use. Lance has requested you and Mrs. Bates come up here for a conversation."

Philip stood up in excitement. "I *knew* she was up to something!"

"She has indeed been very busy it seems. Can you get her up here?"

"I can do my best. Will you send coordinates? We only have standard space cars with the agency."

"We'll come into the system then. I'll send coordinates when we get there."

"Okay, great. How long do you think?"

"Twelve hours max. Probably less. I'll keep you posted."

"Great. I'll need time to coordinate persuading Carol."

"I understand. I hear she has some personal problems with the general."

"Yes. Something like that. Don't worry. I can make it happen. I'll stand by for your ETA and coordinates."

"Very good. ArchAngel out."

And with that, the line disconnected, and the red holoscreen folded itself up back into Philip's holo. He sat back down, contemplating how on Esataria he was going to pull this off.

Aboard *The Empress*

Molly's thoughts tripped idly around her mind as she used the downtime to rest. Her brain felt frazzled from the emotional pressure of the last several days, and though she was always in stressful situations, this was certainly different.

On so many levels.

Oz ventured to talk to her again, now that everything seemed to be under control.

You doing okay?

Yeah. What's up?

Well, since your endorphins and cortisol levels seemed to have returned to normal, I wondered if we might talk about these potential cyber attacks.

What?

Remember? The probes I've been detecting and fending off my most used hubs down on Estaria.

Oh. Shit. Yeah, sorry Oz. It completely went from my mind since Sean disappeared.

It's okay. I understand not everyone has super-enhanced capacity courtesy of the Federation.

Molly smiled to herself. She glanced over at Joel to see if he was reacting to her, but his eyes were closed and his chair tipped back.

So, where are we with it?

Well, I just got another alert that another server was being probed. Not hacked. Just that someone is probably monitoring the in and outflow of packets from it.

What can that tell them?

Not much. Other than there *is* data flowing. If they're able to track the data, that may become an issue. But I'm taking precautions, and since we're going to be out of range anyway, it's not going to be an issue until we get back.

But it's good for us to consider it now?

Yes.

So, who would want to track the data and not interpret it?

I've yet to ascertain that. Judging by the methods they're using, it doesn't look like it's any run of the mill type of hackers. I'm ruling out corporates, lone rangers, and kids. It's far too subtle for that.

So, who does that leave?

Maybe foreign intelligence. But you'd think they'd be a bit more brazen in trying to get whatever they're after. The only other party that we're aware of who might have these kinds of capabilities would be Estarian local intelligence.

You mean Estarian domestic spies?

Exactly.

Molly's brow creased up. *That's... odd.*

Yeah. But it's not as if we haven't been causing a stir in their systems, the medical companies, their financial systems. Plus, they could easily have seen our influence on those subsidiaries that you took control of. That's not including the university.

So, you're saying that whoever is paying attention will likely be aware of all of these different projects?

Unfortunately, yes. They've shown up at about twenty percent of the servers and hubs that I've used for moving or extracting data. Despite my attempts to silo our operations, they're either monitoring the whole Estarian network or...

Or?

They have a beat on my fingerprint. The syntax of the code that I use.

How can they do that?

It's not hard once you've got a big enough sample. It would be like taking a big ass sample of Hemingway and being able to compare it to Dickens and Dostoyevsky. There are tells. Isolate the tells, and then it's easy to scan for those combinations.

Shit. Can you try and hide it? Like modulate your style?

I could. Maybe. But it will take me maybe ten times longer to process anything out there.

Well, maybe we need to do that just to be careful. Remind me to have us circle back to this when we get back to base.

Okay.

Molly sat mulling the issue for some time. Joel stirred next to her. He stretched and then brought his chair upright.

"You okay?" he asked.

Molly blurted out the exact thought that was on her mind. "Why would covert ops on Estaria care about what we're doing?"

"What do you mean? What's going on?"

"Oz and I were talking about the strange probing that has been going on around his hubs planet-side. They stopped for a while, but then he just got an alert again."

Joel rubbed his eyes, thinking. "You don't think it could just be routine?"

Molly shook her head. "Doesn't feel like it. Plus, it doesn't account for how we've had twenty percent of our hubs looked at."

"So, we're being targeted?"

"Yeah. Oz thinks the only folks with the tech to do what they're doing are local clandestine services."

Joel shifted in his seat. "Odd. You think someone is still after you?"

Molly shrugged. "Everyone that was a threat thinks that I'm dead."

Joel nodded. "Yeah. Everyone on Estaria. Except anyone associated with the university."

Molly stopped. "Good point… and good luck controlling that can of worms. But we've taken precautions there, and both Oz and ArchAngel are keeping an eye on factions that might want to attack. They just don't have this kind of access to tech, though. The only other people would be my parents. But the tech thing holds there too, of course."

Joel chuckled. "True. Though I don't see them wanting to probe your missions. I mean, it's not like they work for the military or anything, right?"

"Well, no, of course not." Molly sighed. "I mean, they wouldn't know what a mission was, but…"

Joel detected an unease in her tone. "What is it?"

"Well, you don't know my mom. If she wants to know what I'm up to, she'd go to extraordinary lengths."

"Yeah, but she doesn't have these kinds of capabilities."

"True." Molly smiled. "Yeah. No, of course not. That would be silly."

Joel chuckled. "I'm sure you're just worrying about nothing. And Oz is going to be able to block these advances, right?"

Molly nodded definitely. "Yeah. Already done."

"Okay. So nothing to worry about." Joel settled back into his chair and closed his eyes again. "I'm sure whoever it is will lose interest. And if they don't, we'll find them when we get back."

"Yeah. Okay." Molly looked out of the window again. "I'm sure it's nothing."

Aboard *The Empress*

Several hours had passed since the team had departed Gaitune. They'd been navigating their way from one waypoint coordinate to another, retracing Scamp's steps for any kind of clue.

So far nothing had turned up to leave them any wiser.

Crash brought *The Empress* to a halt at another set of coordinates and then dropped his hands from the controls. He turned his head to look at Pieter.

Pieter felt his frustration and put one finger up. "Okay. Gimme a minute here. I'm working as fast as I can."

Brock noticed Crash's impatience. Although he didn't protest or complain, Brock could tell he was getting tired of having to pull up every so often.

Brock tried to get his attention, but Crash's gaze remained on the hardworking Pieter and his multiple holoscreens he'd set up in an array over one of the rear consoles. Finally, he resigned himself to speaking. "Dude. Can I get you a mocha or something while we wait?"

Crash didn't move. "No thanks."

"Well… why don't you have a walk? Stretch your legs?"

Crash sighed, looked out at the starscape on the main screen, then heaved himself up. "Fine," he agreed. He wandered out of the cockpit, glancing at the holoscreens as he wandered past Pieter.

"You're doing great," Brock whispered to Pieter. "He just gets grouchy when he's tired and not making progress."

Pieter glanced up briefly and smiled before continuing what he was doing on the screens. He looked like he was working under pressure. Brock sat back in his own chair, leaving him to get on with it.

Just then, a quiet alert activated on his console. Emma's voice chirped up. "Brock, it's Giles again. He's calling from *The Scamp Princess*, in flight on a course to the Ferrai Quadrant."

"Ferrai Quadrant? That guy gets around. Okay, cool. Put him through." Brock waited to hear the line shift before he spoke. "Hey, Giles?"

"Hi. Brock, right?"

"Yeah. How you doing?"

"All good, thanks. How are you?"

"Doing all right. You wanna speak to Molly again?"

Giles's voice faltered. "Erm, yeah—No. Not necessary. If you don't mind passing on a message that is…"

Brock and Pieter exchanged a brief glance before Brock responded. "Sure. No problem. Shoot." Brock leaned forward, his elbows on the arms of the chair, listening intently.

"It's Anne," Giles explained. "I thought Molly should know. She snuck aboard *The Scamp Princess* and is now on the mission with us."

Brock burst out laughing. "You're kidding? You've got a stowaway?" he confirmed.

"I wish I *were* kidding."

"Oh man. Shit. I'm sorry."

"Yeah. Thanks."

"So, how the fuck did this happen?" Brock asked.

They heard Giles sigh heavily on the other end of the line. "Well, it seems—and Emma may be able to help with this—but from what Paige could figure out, our little Estarian friend is actually capable of fuzzing out her own image on cameras and electronic feeds."

"No shit!"

"I shit you not."

"Fuck," Brock said. "So, this is going to be an issue."

"Potentially. I recommended putting a bell around her neck. Arlene didn't go for it, but I think after a few days, she may come around to the suggestion."

"Wow. Okay. I'll let Molly know. Obviously, nothing we can do about it yet, but…"

"Of course," Giles said. "We'll keep her safe and bring her home soon."

"Cool. Thanks for letting us know, Giles. All the best juju with your mission!"

"Thanks, Brock," Giles responded. "You too."

The line disconnected. Pieter looked up from his screens. "What was that?"

"Giles." Brock chuckled. "Apparently, Anne slipped out on *The Scamp Princess* with him." Brock shook his head. "That girl… I gotta go tell Mollz."

Pieter's eyes were back on his screens. "Aight," he muttered absently.

Brock wandered into the lounge. The atmosphere was still pretty tense and quiet as a library. Jack was napping. Joel was playing video games on his wrist holo.

Molly was sitting near the front, looking out of the window.

He approached her gently, as if approaching a wild horse that might bolt at a sudden movement.

"Hey," he said quietly.

Molly's head turned, and her eyes locked on to his. "Hey, Brock. How's it going?"

"It's going good. Pieter's doing a great job up there. We're making progress."

"Good." She forced a smile.

"I've just taken a call from Giles, though," he added, his face a little more serious. He felt Molly's defenses go up as she braced herself.

"What did he say?"

Joel wandered over to hear the conversation. He stopped a row of seats back and leaned his arms over on the back of one as he listened. Brock glanced at him before he continued. "Everything is okay. It turns out that Anne was missing, but she's shown up on Giles's ship."

Molly took a second to react. "You're kidding?"

Brock pressed his lips together and shook his head once. "That was what I said."

Joel scoffed. "Son of a—" His shock turned to half a laugh, which turned to a cough.

Brock bobbed his head, trying to keep his face straight.

"How?" Molly asked.

Brock took a breath to compose himself and then slowly exhaled. "It sounds like we have a bigger security issue, to be honest."

Molly cocked her head questioningly.

"Seems our teenager with woo woo superpowers is able to fuzz out her image on the base cameras."

Joel was still chuckling and coping with his shock. "You know, I bet if she can get past those, she can probably get past any cameras."

Molly bobbed her head. "I'm thinking keeping tabs on her is going to be much harder than we first thought." She glanced at Joel. "Kinda like bottling lightning."

Joel raised his eyebrows. "I'd say."

Molly frowned and looked back to Brock. "Okay, well, we'll have to figure out a way around this, or a way to make her stay put and keep her safe—"

"And we need to figure out who is after her," Joel interjected.

"Right," Molly agreed quickly. "But in the meantime, if Giles is keeping an eye on her, then we can only hope for the best."

"Right, cool," Brock agreed, starting to leave. "He said he would. And if he can, of course, he will. I'll have a chat with Emma and see what we can do about modifying the cameras or something." He shook his head, his eyes betraying his amazement. "I still can't believe it."

Molly shook her head in sympathy. "I know, right? Kids!"

Joel chuckled and patted Molly on her shoulder as he also turned to go. "I hear it's different when they're your own, though."

"Ha!" Molly snorted. "You can't just hand them back when they're your own. I have trouble remembering to feed a cat, remember?"

Brock chuckled as he disappeared out of the door. Joel headed back to his seat, leaving Molly still shaking her head.

Shit.

What's up, Oz?

That's my fault. I should have been on to her.

There's no way—

How I could have known? Yes, there was. I totally should have known. And from the sounds of it, Paige figured it out. How did Paige figure it out, and I didn't catch it?

Hey, listen to me. You were working on the task at hand: finding Sean. There was no way any of us could have predicted what Anne would be capable of. Or what she might do. Remember, we barely know her yet.

Well, I've obviously been compiling my own heuristic of her.

And how's that going?

Well, no clear guidelines. Nothing of any significance anyway. She barely talks to anyone. She doesn't reveal things about herself. She spends a lot of time out of the way of the

cameras in her room. There are a few data points but no patterns to tell us anything.

Yeah. I think when we get back, we need to put some effort into correcting that.

Okay. I'll make it my priority.

Oz. Stop. You're fretting. She's safe right now. With Giles. You didn't screw up.

Well, why do I feel like I did?

Erm, maybe because you're a perfectionist?

I'm not. That's a wholly human quality.

Oh, and feelings aren't? Tendencies aren't? Humor isn't?

Okay. Touché.

Good. Now stop beating yourself up and get back to helping Pieter figure out where we need to be and whose ass we need to kick!

Yes, ma'am.

Molly sniggered quietly and leaned her head back and closed her eyes. She could always count on her team and best friend to make her feel better, no matter what was going on.

CHAPTER FOUR

Paige's office, safe house, Gaitune-67

The office was relatively quiet. Since the debacle with Anne stealing away, it was just Paige and Maya on the base now.

And Bourne.

But Bourne didn't really count, Paige mused to herself in the silence. He mostly kept to himself, churning away on the redundant processing power that sat within the confines of the base firewall.

It was a good opportunity to catch up on some work. Paige had hunkered down in her office, mocha machine keeping her adequately caffeinated to deal with the load.

She looked at the time. She hadn't moved for two hours and hadn't been outside or in any kind of simulated daylight since she got up. Then, she realized she hadn't showered since yesterday, either.

She pushed back in her chair, sighing. She still had a heap of stuff to do. But she needed a break.

Just then, her desk holo pinged. It was a comm from an address she didn't recognize. It looked official. She scooted her chair closer to the holoscreen to read it. It was about the university.

Her decision to take a break forgotten, she poked her finger into the hologram and opened the message. Her tired eyes darted left and right, assimilating the information.

Her stomach lurched.

She sat back, her mind reeling from the information. *She should call Molly.*

But Molly was probably out of range now.

ADAM.

Nope. ADAM was out of range.

ArchAngel? Well, she is obviously the next best thing, but she wasn't interested in university problems.

Her mind flicked to Gareth. He'd warned her months ago that something like this might be coming. She'd dismissed it. And him. Things hadn't ended well, and his warning had only served to show her how much she didn't trust him.

She wiped her face with her hands.

If in doubt, do nothing, she told herself.

She'd go shower. And then talk to Maya about it. It wasn't within Maya's official remit to get involved in university stuff, but still, she was a good friend. And had a good head on her shoulders. They'd figure it out together.

She scooted her chair back again and hit save on the message so she could find it easily from her wrist holo later. Then she got up and left the office, flicking the mocha machine off as she went.

Aboard *The Empress*

Brock arrived back in the cockpit to find Crash perched on the navigation console, his eyes glazed over and looking at the floor.

"You'll never guess what's happened," Brock announced as he

strode in and collapsed into his console chair. "Woo woo voodoo teenager strikes again!"

Crash looked up. "Who? Anne?"

"Yeah."

"Why? What's she done now?"

"Oh, you know," Brock explained mock-casually, "only gone and bypassed the entire base technology and snuck away on *The Scamp Princess* with Giles."

"No way!" Crash exclaimed, his expression verging on surprised.

"Way."

"Oh, man. That's… intense. How did Oz take it?"

Brock shrugged. "Dunno. I only spoke to Molly."

Pieter looked up. "From what I can tell, he's not taking it well. His processing has slowed down by fifty percent since you headed out there to tell her."

Crash sniggered. "Well, well, well. AIs suffer from pride."

Brock grinned. "Appears so. But seriously, this could be a problem. If she's deliberately doing it to hide herself, that's one thing. I mean, we don't think she wants to screw us over. But what about if she's doing it accidentally, and it leaves us vulnerable?"

Crash had folded his arms and was stroking his chin with his fingers on one hand. "You have a point. And to take this one step further, what else is she compromising?"

Brock sighed and swiveled a console chair around to sit on. "Who knows? I mean, one problem at a time, but when we get back, we're going to have our hands full trying to woo woo-proof the base."

Crash closed his eyes. "Crap. You're right."

Brock spun round and started punching keys in the holos at the console. "I'm gonna see if Emma and I can get a jump on anything that might help while you guys are finding out where we need to be." He spun back to address Pieter. "Lemme know if you need me on anything else, though. I'm right here, yeah?"

Pieter stopped typing to respond. "Sure thing. Thanks, man."

"Any time, brooooooooo..." he called, turning his music on via his holo for his audio implant.

Crash sighed and slumped down in his pilot's chair, wishing he could just fly.

Paige's quarters, Safehouse, Gaitune-67

Paige stepped out of the shower and wrapped herself in the self-drying towel. Then she grabbed a second one and wrapped her hair in it.

She padded out to the bedroom and set about moisturizing and dressing.

"Paige?" It was a computerized voice over the comm system.

Paige froze, confused. Oz was away. And it didn't seem like Oz. A second later, she realized it was Bourne.

"Bourne. Hi. What's up?" She clutched her towel around her tighter.

"I was checking incoming messages and noticed you weren't at your desk to receive yours at the moment."

"Yes..." she said slowly, still bamboozled why Bourne was monitoring messages or needed to tell her about it.

"Well, there was one that seemed out of place. So, I figured it might be important. It's about your company."

"Oh, is that right?"

"Seems someone wants to buy it."

Paige paused again, deodorant only under one arm. "I see."

"Do you want me to send it through to your holo?"

"Yes, please." She finished putting her deodorant on and hurriedly pulled on her underwear and sweats.

"Bourne?" she asked, feeling a little less vulnerable now she was dressed.

"Yes, Paige?"

"How come you're monitoring messages?"

"I was bored with the archives. I wanted a break. And it seemed like a sensible thing to do since you guys aren't monitoring anything at the moment. Good job, too. Else you would have experienced a time lag in your communications about this important message."

Paige raised an eyebrow comically. She didn't know whether to chuckle or be annoyed at him. "Okay. Thanks so much, Bourne. But you really don't need to worry about monitoring our communications. Most of it isn't time sensitive, and we have protocols in place for when it is."

"Oh, okay then," he responded flatly.

The intercom went quiet. Paige sensed she was alone again. For the first time in her years in the safe house, she was glad there weren't cameras in the quarters. That would have just been… creepy.

She headed back into the bathroom where she had left her wrist holo on the vanity counter. She strapped it back on and opened her messages. Bourne was right. There was a new one. From another sender she didn't recognize.

Her heart started racing. She prodded the message in the hologram and opened it up. Again, she scanned it. This time, instead of a sinking feeling, she felt anxious and perhaps a little excited.

Her eyes scanned down.

"Fuck me," she muttered to herself. "That is a lot of zeros." She whistled out through her teeth. "Pheeeew!"

Her brain stopped processing properly. She knew she needed to dry her hair and style it, plus a host of other things in her routine, but all she could think about was talking to Maya.

She hit her implant. "Maya? Are you there?"

A moment later, Maya responded. "Yeah, what's up?"

"Someone has just offered me a truckload of money to buy my company. I need a yoll-arita and some girl time."

"Sounds good to me. I'm just finishing up at the gym. Gimme twenty minutes to get showered, and I'll meet you in the kitchen."

"Okay, you're on!" Paige tapped her implant and the call disconnected. She carefully sat back down on the bed, allowing the new reality to sink in.

<u>Bates Residence, Spire, Estaria</u>

The Sark had gone down hours ago. All being well, Philip's wife would be home shortly. She'd messaged him as she was leaving the office. Accounting for traffic, he knew it would be less than three minutes. Plenty of time to make the call.

"Yes, she's here. No problem. You can give the boys a night off. I'm taking her on a trip off-world, so she won't need protection. Great. Thanks, Jack. You have a good night, too."

Philip hung up the call on the secure holo console in the living room.

That took care of the security detail. Now, he just needed to make sure that everything else went smoothly.

He waited in the living room patiently. He'd done this a million times before, albeit never to his wife.

The front door opened. He heard her high heels click against the polished floorboards in the hallway. He heard her place her things down on the floor. Her heard her take her atmos jacket off and then pick up her things and head into the—

"Hello, dear." He smiled congenially.

"Hello, Philip. How was your day?" She looked frazzled. This might screw up his plan.

"Oh, can't complain," he said brightly. "Fancy heading out for dinner tonight?"

She cocked her head and smiled. "Err, yeah. Sure. That would be... lovely."

"Good." Philip grinned, getting up. "How about we leave in say, ten minutes?"

"Okay, fine. Let me just head upstairs for a few."

"Okay, dear, no need to change," he added. "We'll go somewhere fairly casual, if that suits you?"

"Yes, fine," she said, her mood clearly lifted by the prospect of a break from the old routine. She trotted up the stairs, leaving her shoes at the bottom so she could move more easily.

Philip hummed to himself, monitoring his own heartbeat in his chest. He was indeed nervous. The chances of getting this wrong were always high. Which, of course, meant that things had the potential to get messy. Which was the last thing he wanted in his own home. But then… orders were orders.

He continued to hum as he prepared the things he needed. He ambled over to the kitchen and opened up the main drawer, pulling out some cable ties. He very deliberately placed them down on the counter, next to the plant so it wasn't obvious they were there. Then he moved to another drawer by the oven and pulled out the auto-syringe that he'd prepared earlier that afternoon. All he needed was to get it onto a vein, and the machine would do the rest.

He placed it into his pants pocket and then ambled back to the living room. He heard her moving around upstairs. After a few moments, she seemed to be coming back down. He waited for her to nearly reach the bottom before he started moving back toward the hallway door. She was hurrying, putting in earrings and then rummaging in her bag at the bottom of the stairs.

"I can't find my lipstick," she muttered.

"Take your time, dear," he cooed, leaning against the doorframe, watching her carefully like a cat watched a canary in a cage. Cool. Confident. He waited, as if just waiting for the perfect note in the music, fully aware of when it was going to come.

Carol moved from the bag and started heading toward him and into the open-plan living area. As she walked past him, in one swift movement, he put his arm out to stop her moving and with the other, jabbed the syringe to her neck.

For a second, she called out as if pleasantly surprised by his advance. Her face quickly turned to one of horror as she felt the jabbing pain in her neck. She turned, looking at him with utter betrayal, unable to move or do anything about what had just happened.

And then she slumped in his arms. He caught her and laid her down gently. Then he reached for the cable ties and started binding her wrists and ankles.

Kitchen, Safehouse, Gaitune-67

Maya was already in the kitchen by the time Paige emerged from her rushed beauty routine. Maya hadn't bothered to dry her hair. Being full-blood Estarian, she didn't have the problems Paige had with it going frizzy if she didn't dry it after a shower.

"Yoll-aritas are up in three minutes. I've got some snacks in the oven."

Paige grinned. "You're an ascended one, you are!"

Maya turned over her shoulder. "I know. I just need to put in a petition with the Ancestors to recognize that!"

Paige chuckled and sat down at the table, still cooling off from the shower. "You know, it's kinda neat to remember my Estarian roots."

Maya continued to pour ingredients into the cocktail shaker. "You feel like it's all a bit too human up here?"

"Sometimes."

Maya giggled. "And this coming from the half-human. You've got to appreciate the irony of that!" She turned over her shoulder again and winked at Paige before grabbing some glasses and pouring their yoll-aritas. She plonked the full glasses on the table, glanced at the oven timer, and then sat down.

Paige took one of the glasses and Maya the other. Paige grinned. "To some decent girl time!"

Maya smiled. "I'll drink to that!" They clinked their glasses and took a sip, savoring the moment like a sacred ceremonial act. Then, quietly, they both replaced their glasses on the table and paused.

"On my ancestors," Maya started excitedly, "what's this about selling your company?"

Paige's eyes lit up, and the girls started talking animatedly. "You won't believe it. It's just come from out of the blue. Some holding company has approached me and wants to buy the whole organization. For cash!"

"My word! Who has that much cash?" Maya took another sip of her drink.

Paige shrugged, pulling up her holo to show Maya the message. "Says it's from Info Corp. I've not done a search yet to find out who they are. I'm just in a daze from it all."

Maya scanned the holoscreen Paige had pushed over to her. She shook her head in amazement. "Who'd have thought, eh? I mean, wow!"

"Right?"

Maya sighed and sat back in her chair. "What are you going to do?"

"No idea. I can't think straight at the moment. Plus, there are so many questions I have before I can even begin to make a decision about this."

Maya nodded quietly, allowing Paige the space to talk it out.

"I mean," Paige continued, "we always knew the day would come where I would have to make a big decision like this. And the bigger the company got, the more likely it was that I was going to have to choose between the mission and the company." She bobbed her head to one side and continued to play with the stem of her glass. "Then there's the added pressure of the university."

Maya took another slurp of her drink. "There's no doubt you've been juggling a lot."

Paige stuck her bottom lip out. "This is true. Although in terms of actual stuff that I have to do, the teams handle that. I mostly just have to make decisions. That's all."

"Head space, though," Maya pointed out.

"True."

The girls sat in silence for a moment, contemplating all the variables.

"You know," Maya piped up, "I wonder who this company is." She pulled up her holo and ran a basic search.

Paige's eyes had already glazed over.

"Info Corp, here we go," Maya read off. "Looks like they're the same holding company that bought up Newstainment a few months ago."

Paige's face registered a flicker of recognition. "So, why would they be interested in my company?"

Maya pressed her lips together as she opened a couple more holoscreens. "You know, I'm not entirely sure. It looks like these other companies are all in the media and communications sector."

Paige regarded Maya over her glass as she drank to quiet her confusion. "You think they're after my customer list?"

Maya sighed. "Maybe. I mean, it's a big-ass customer database. Plus, factor in all the big data your marketing department has collected: all segmented, tagged, and pulling like gang busters."

"How would they know that's what we were doing?"

Maya shrugged. "Having a drink with one of your team down on Estaria would reveal that kind of thing in half an hour."

Paige nodded, her mind churning. "I guess they would see from the accounts the profit and then be able to work back to the amount of profit we're generating per data point."

Maya sighed. "Quite easily, I would think. I mean, don't get me wrong. It's an amazing product. And to build something over three systems to millions of credits per annum, it's phenomenal. No one expected that. But I doubt they're buying you for the revenue."

"You mean they're after the infrastructure?"

"Yeah. And maybe the secret source you have in getting your product under the right noses. The database is only part of the asset."

Paige's eyes were focused off in the distance. Somewhere beyond even the kitchen wall. "Wow. This is… a turn out for the books."

"It's pretty impressive," Maya agreed. "You should be super proud of what you've achieved."

Paige laughed dryly and wiped her hand back across her forehead to her hair before resting her arm on the table with her head in her hand. "Yeah, if there was ever any time to sit back and smell the roses!"

Maya gave her a knowing look. "Maybe this is an opportunity to do that, then?" She paused. "How long is the offer on the table?" She nodded at Paige's holo for the information.

"Two weeks," Paige replied without needing to check.

"Well, we have a little time."

Paige nodded her head slowly and repeatedly. "Okay, tomorrow we work on this."

Maya pressed her lips together again. "Sure. Probably worth using the base facilities, too. I'd like to do some stealthy digging on this. Something's niggling me."

Paige frowned. "Yeah, me too. I mean, Newstainment? Something tells me we're going to need access to all the resources we can get on this one if we're going to get to the bottom of what's going on."

Maya narrowed her eyes. "You're suspecting something?"

Paige almost grimaced. "Between this and the government move on the university, I think we'd be naive to rule anything out at this stage."

Maya's eyebrows darted to the top of her face. "The university? What's going on there?" The tone of Paige's voice had her alarmed.

Paige took another long sip of her drink. "Well, I kinda knew something was coming. Gareth warned me the other week. But we didn't know quite what form it was going to take. Plus, from past history, he's not the most reliable source."

"What do you mean? What's coming?"

"I received a notification from some government division about some bullshit health and safety review that the university is under."

"Why? What for?"

"From what Gareth was saying, someone in the government is out to shut us down. I dismissed it at the time because it was coming from him. I figured, why was he just telling me? If it were genuine, he has protocols with Molly to alert the team. But he didn't. I figured it was just a ruse to get talking again."

"So, you ignored it?"

"Yeah. And then I got this holocomm from the board of health and safety."

Paige pulled up another holocomm she'd received that afternoon. She flushed as the anxiety flooded through her body again.

Maya read the comm and then pushed it back toward her. "Shit. That looks…"

"Serious?" Paige said grimly. "Yeah, you're telling me."

"No wonder you needed a drink," Maya said sympathetically. "So, what are you going to do?"

Paige's face fell, and her shoulders rolled over. She rested both arms on the table. "I dunno yet. Molly left me in charge. I suppose it needs handling. But I'm not really sure what we can do."

Maya took a deep breath, then stood up to check the oven. "Okay, well, who might know?" she probed.

Paige thought for a moment before her eyes lit up. "Ah! Yes!

Good point. Gareth. The guy who helped us set up the institution in the first place. He's got a good idea about rules and regulations. Let me message him."

Paige typed quickly on her holo, hoping that the alcohol wasn't influencing her just yet. She hit send. "Okay, we're fixing an appointment to talk tomorrow. Hopefully, he'll be able to give me a hand."

Maya had pulled the snacks out of the oven. "Okay, that's one down. Now what are you going to do about your company?"

Paige's eyes returned to the grim look of dismay. "I have no idea." She sighed. "That's something I can't think about sober." She smiled weakly before raising her half empty glass to Maya.

Maya got the message. "Okay, snacks and drinks. And no more talk of difficult decisions until tomorrow!"

CHAPTER FIVE

<u>Glom Space station, Kirox Quadrant</u>

Four days earlier...

Karina waited for her server to place the mocha she had ordered on her table and then walk away. She pulled up her wrist holo again and reopened the screen. The long-range call was astonishingly still connected.

"I dunno what kind of tech this is," she blurted out in a low voice, "but I know if your government found out..."

Carol Bates leered arrogantly back at her. "Actually Karina, dear, it's your government *too*, remember? And those who need to know are well aware we have it. Our collective job is protecting the planet, and long-range comm technology is hardly a misuse."

Karina's nostrils flared defiantly. "Unless you count harassing people who traveled excruciating distances and even braved cryo-stasis to avoid your interference!"

"Now, now," Carol Bates retorted in a warning tone. "No need to be rude. You may be a long way in terms of light years, but one wrong move, young lady, and I can arrange to have you snapped back in an instant. And if that happens, our deal is off."

"Well, you won't have any need for that, just as long as you keep up your end of the bargain." Karina's tone softened. "I do this, and we both walk. No more bullshit. No more missions. You let us live in peace."

Carol glanced down at her nails and pretended to be disinterested and aloof. "I'll keep my end of the bargain. Though I can't imagine you'll be at peace with that... *man*."

Karina's gaze darted around the area offscreen as she checked the restaurant. She'd deliberately chosen one out of the way so she could prepare in peace. Carol's annoying interruption was ruining that peace now. But she also wanted somewhere that would minimize casualties.

Timing was going to be everything.

"Look," Karina huffed, her gaze snapping back to the holo-screen. "If there's nothing else, some of us have work to do. He's on his way."

Carol raised her hands in a mocking surrender gesture. "Okay, okay. I'll leave you to get on with it. But remember," she looked menacingly into the camera lens, "you fuck this up and you're done."

Karina felt a shudder creeping up her spine. She desperately didn't want Carol to see that she was getting to her, though. She made a conscious effort to maintain her facial expression as best she could and closed the call.

Then she shuddered.

That woman is the biggest bitch I've ever known. I can't imagine what it would be like to be her daughter.

The restaurant door opened and her hired flunky stepped in. Spotting her across the restaurant, he bumbled his way between the rows of empty dining tables, furtively glancing around as he did.

He was clearly packing.

Karina rolled her eyes. "Could you draw any more attention

to yourself?" she asked casually, kicking a chair out on the other side of the table from her. She nodded at it. "Sit."

He pulled the seat out and sat down obediently. This was a man who was used to taking orders.

Karina leaned over the table and spoke slowly and deliberately. "Okay, the beacon has been destroyed, which means that he's on his way here right now."

The flunky nodded.

"So, you know what you need to do?" she asked.

"I sure do. I wait until you give me the signal and then I start firing."

"Yes. In my general direction, but for Ancestor's sake, don't hit me. Or anyone else. Is that clear?"

"Yep. That's clear. I can do that. I once went to shooting practice with the boss and never shot a thing."

Karina was about to continue but halted as she processed what she just heard. She frowned, opened her mouth to speak, and then closed it again.

"Is there anything else Ms. Karina?"

She gathered herself again and moved the mocha cup closer to her. "No, Ronnie. That's everything. But make sure you sell it. And then disappear. I'll do the rest. We just want him to feel like I'm in danger, okay?"

"Yes, Ms. Karina. I can do that."

Karina nodded abruptly once. "Okay," she said definitively. "Go sit over there and order something. And wait for my signal. And for goodness sake, don't keep looking at me… or don't make it look like you're watching me."

"Got it." Ronnie got up and moved to a booth nearer the door where Karina had indicated.

Karina sipped her mocha. She hoped to hell this was going to work because getting Ronnie killed in her little ruse wasn't something she wanted to have to live with.

· · ·

Philip's car, just outside Estarian satellite orbit

Carol found herself in the dark, gradually becoming aware of her surroundings. And a headache to end all headaches.

She shifted herself, feeling a hard surface beneath her. Then she remembered.

Philip!

She struggled, discovering that her wrists were bound.

And her ankles.

"What the—"

Well, at least she wasn't gagged. *"Philip!"* she screamed at the top of her lungs. The board she was lying on moved and she lurched sideways.

Dammit. She was in the trunk of a car. How... amateurish, she thought.

She shuffled around to figure out which way she was facing. She started feeling the outer edges of her space as best she could with her hands bound. Noticing the lull of the car from side to side, she deduced they were already in space. She didn't want to open the trunk in that case.

She shuffled over onto her other side. This would take her into the car. Carefully, she searched with her fingers for the pull switch that would put the back seats down. She knew that if they were in Philip's car, they would go down.

Unless he'd tied them so they wouldn't.

She found the catch and pushed. It moved. She pushed again, using all the might she could muster without putting her foot through the trunk.

The seat back fell forward, letting light into her little cubby hole.

"You fucking arsewipe!" she screamed into the car. "What the fuck are you doing?"

She started clambering into the main compartment of the car, her headache only exasperating her foul mood now.

"Oh, you're awake," Philip said casually. "Hello, dear."

"Don't you 'hello dear,' me. What the fuck?"

Philip watched her struggling through the back of the car in his rearview mirror. "It's the only way I could get you to come with me."

"Why?" she demanded. "Where are you taking me?"

"To someone who can talk some sense into you."

"What are you talking about?" She fell inelegantly forward into the footwell of the opposite side of the car, dragging her bound legs behind her.

Philip kept his face straight, knowing full well he would never hear the end of it if he started laughing at her now. "Lance has requested a meeting with us," he said simply.

"That pompous asshole!" She elbowed her way back up onto the seat. "He doesn't need a reason to throw his so-called authority around. Just because he has bigger guns and alien tech doesn't mean he gets to boss the rest of the world around."

"Actually, it does," Philip corrected her.

Carol finally managed to swing her legs down and sat herself up, bringing her eyes up to the mirror to glare at her traitorous husband. A thought occurred to her. "It was *you* who had been accessing my files!"

"And ADAM," Philip confessed. "Seems someone has been a very bad girl." His tone changed to something rather seductive.

Under any other circumstances, Carol knew she would respond differently. Right now, though, he was in the dog house.

"I have been no such thing!" she said angrily.

"Right. And that is why I've had orders to get you up there?"

There was a pause as Carol fumed in the back seat, coming to terms with the inevitability of the meeting.

"Anyway," Philip said, keeping the tone light, "you should probably know before we get up there, there's been a problem. They've lost Sean."

"Well, that's no big loss," Carol chuffed.

"And Molly's gone after him," Philip added.

Carol Bates turned instantly pale.

"Anything you want to share, Carol? Before you have to confess your sins to the big guy?"

Carol was silent for a moment, her anger diffusing right in front of Philip's eyes. She hesitated before responding. "No. Nothing."

"Are you sure?" he pressed. "Because this has Carol Bates, Head of Estarian Clandestine Operations, written all over it." He added, "I know my wife."

Her eyes flicked away from the mirror and fixed on something outside one of the windows. "Well," she said slowly, thinking as fast as she could, "I might have arranged to have Sean lured out to another sector."

"How?"

"An old operative. Someone who has history with him."

Philip closed his eyes briefly in frustration before searching for her gaze again. "What exactly did you do?"

"I just encouraged her to get him away from this system and..." She paused again.

"And what?" Philip demanded.

She coughed a little before she responded. "Marry him."

"What the *fuck*, Carol? Are you fucking insane?" The car swerved off track, and the auto-navigation started beeping loudly.

"Careful!" Carol shouted back. "You'll get us killed, you crazy old goat!"

Philip reset the steering and flicked the alarm off. He shook his head, composing himself outwardly, but clearly still seething. "You're the one that's going to get our daughter killed."

Carol didn't respond. She had gone into sulking mode. He recognized it well from the myriad of tiny facial cues she gave off.

The worst thing to do now would be not to keep her talking. If she was talking, she could be brought around. If she was left to sulk, the issue would fester and would no doubt blow up in a bigger problem very soon. "How on Estaria is getting some operative to marry him a good thing to do?" he asked, incredulous but not as angry now.

Carol seemed to return to logic, which was better than sulking, but dangerous territory for him. "Well, then it means he's unavailable… and won't get any more involved with Molly. I want him as far away from her as possible."

"By getting him hitched?"

"Well, I didn't know she'd go after him!" she protested, as if that were the issue they were debating.

"Of course, she's going to go after him if she thinks he's in danger. Which is clearly what's happened if he's gone dark. This is what teams do for each other. If you'd spent more than five minutes in the field, relying on anyone but yourself, you'd know that already."

Silence hung in the air of the tiny space car.

Her face changed. If she didn't have her wrists bound, Philip knew she'd be folding her arms right about now. He needed to keep her talking, even if they were arguing. "I mean, in what world is getting him married off a logical way to protect Molly?" he muttered, only half expecting an answer this time.

Her jawline hardened. Back to logic. "Look," she said matter-of-factly. "Since we're already en route, how about you undo these ties and let me sit up front?"

"No fucking way!" he said immediately. "You're staying back there. Tied up. I wasn't born yesterday."

"But I'm your wife! You can't treat me like this!"

"And as your husband, I'm doing damage control. And that means stopping you from doing anything else that could put our daughter in jeopardy."

"Hmpft," she scoffed. "You could have at least used the newer ones that don't chafe the skin."

Philip ignored her and glared into the blackness of space ahead of them, his eyes scanning for signs of *The ArchAngel*.

The sooner they got on board, the better.

Glom Space station, Kirox Quadrant

Karina glanced nervously at her holo. She was on her second mocha, and Ronnie seemed to be halfway through some kind of fry-up.

For the umpteenth time, the restaurant door opened, pulling her attention and pushing her into high alert. A small Ogg-like lady walked in and called something to the server behind the bar, who replied back. She strode hurriedly across the room.

Staff, Karina decided. She went back to her mocha.

Just then, the door went again, and again, her heartbeat doubled, giving her a shot of adrenaline through her system. It was a tall, broad human. Karina's emotions recognized the face before her mind did.

This was it!

She glanced anxiously at Ronnie, suddenly wishing she hadn't created this setup. Sean moved one step into the restaurant and locked eyes with her immediately.

She froze.

Her mind spun with all the things she wanted to tell him. All the regrets and hopes she had had over the years. She willed him to come closer. To not look so intense. She couldn't read him. Was he mad at her? Was it because she wasn't in bindings that he figured she wasn't in trouble? Or was this just him in high alert?

Then, everything started to happen in slow motion. She was vaguely aware of a figure moving off to his right. Sean was onto it fast. He knew there was a threat. What did she expect?

She called out to him. This wasn't how it was supposed to go down.

Ronnie fired in her direction. She ducked, her hands automatically coming up to cover her face.

"That was too close!" she shouted, forgetting the ruse. But Ronnie was gone and out on the veranda of the restaurant, scrambling back down into the walkway of the station's main thoroughfare.

Sean took half a second to glare at her before he was off like a shot, chasing Ronnie through the crowded road.

Shaking, Karina sat back down. She needed to wait for him to come back. This was the point. Not for her to run around like the more-than-capable spy she had become.

Damsel in distress. That was what had brought them together in the first place. That was what she needed to be.

She reached for her mocha. Her hand was already steadying itself. Five years out of it, but somehow, it felt a lot like riding an anti-grav bike.

Just then, two rather large humans strode confidently into the restaurant. They were well dressed and muscly. Probably enhanced with cyborg-tech. Top of the line if her estimation about their movements was correct.

She watched them approach her before suddenly realizing they weren't part of her plan, and there was nothing to say they were with Sean. Their expressions looked too determined.

Her brain finally clicked into gear. "Hello, boys. You looking for someone?"

"Yeah. You by the looks of it, princess!"

"Well," she said, keeping her cool and gently getting to her feet. "I'm afraid I'm going to have to disappoint you." She waited until they were two steps from her table and gently reached down as casually as if she were picking up her purse. Instead, she put her fingers under the edge of the table and, in one swift movement, flipped it up into them.

The movement, more than the table, stopped them in their tracks.

Karina reached for her pistol strapped to her leg and started firing. A second later, her arm was in a lock, one of the men having grabbed it and taken her gun right out of her hand. She struggled, pulling sharply to free herself. But she couldn't move.

"Damn fucking cyborgs!" she screamed in frustration.

She reached into her jacket pocket for her handheld stunner. All she needed to do was press one side of it onto one of the guys, and he'd go down. Then she could fight her way out. She got her fingers onto it in the pocket and then felt a sharp pain in the side of her neck.

A second later, her arms and legs went numb.

"Sorry, princess," she heard the gruff voice gloating. "Someone important wants to see you."

Then, everything felt hazy before her vision blacked out.

She was down.

Aboard *The ArchAngel*, undisclosed location

The door swished open, and Lance hauled himself up from his console in his private study. He arrived in his main office to see Barb readjusting the portrait on his wall.

"Barb!" he called amicably. "Thank you for coming so quickly."

"No problem, boss. Anything I can do to help."

"I'm glad you said that." He paused, letting it sink in. "This is a little out of your normal operational scope, I'm afraid. But I'd very much appreciate your help."

Barb stepped away from the picture she'd been adjusting and, satisfied it was now straight, wandered over to the sofa area where Lance was inviting her to sit.

"It's also rather delicate," he added.

Barb smiled confidently. "Which is why you needed a woman's touch."

"Something like that," he admitted, sitting down at one corner.

"So, what gives?" she asked, sitting down on the sofa around the corner from him.

"You remember Carol Bates? Head of clandestine operations down on Estaria?"

"Boy, do I. That woman—"

Lance held his hand up to silence her. "I know. But the less said…"

Barb pressed her lips together and nodded.

Lance continued. "So, she's on her way up here."

Barb frowned. "Oh? We're in the Sark System?"

Lance smiled. "Yes. You missed the announcements?"

"I guess," she said sheepishly. "I've had my head in some research for Frank. Trying to get done before we take a break together."

"I see."

"Yeah, anyway," she continued, staying completely focused on the point. "What do you need me to do? Babysit her while she's on board?"

Lance took a deep breath. "Actually, it's more than that."

Barb raised her eyebrows.

Lance looked serious. "I need you to get her talking. Find out everything she's been up to. Sean's gone missing, and she's got something to do with it."

Barb frowned. "Don't you have people who can do this kind of… interrogation?"

"Yes, but, well… Carol is the mother of one of our best assets in this system. And well, there's a bigger picture."

"How so?"

"Well, I think we all know that Carol's issue with the Federation is very specific. But she and her department have a lot to offer. I'm afraid big things are coming for this little system, and it won't be long before it's going to need to make a decision about joining the Federation officially… or fending for itself. Obviously, if it chooses to go against us, that will have implications."

Barb nodded slowly. "So, you're thinking if we can get her on our side, we can influence things to bring them into the fold gently?"

"Exactly."

Barb narrowed her eyes and regarded the young-looking general carefully. "What else aren't you telling me?"

"Well, there are specific threats I think she'll be helpful on. But she doesn't have that level of clearance. I only want to loop her in if we know she's coming on board. And the other complication is her daughter."

Barb frowned. "Why? What about her?"

"We have reason to suspect they have a strained relationship," Lance disclosed. "Very little contact. Not quite sure what's gone on there. But we need her to align with her daughter, so we need that mess fixed, too."

Barb shook her head and breathed out rapidly. "Wow. You don't ask for much, do you? You realize I'm not a trained psychologist or anything?"

"Yes, Barb, I know that. But if you're able to talk Frank around and keep Giles in line long enough to survive puberty, I think you can talk Carol round."

Lance shifted on the sofa as if to get up, then changed his mind. "Oh, and one more thing. Turns out she's pretty talkative when she's had a few martinis." He shrugged. "God knows how she became a spy with that issue, but…"

Barb sniggered. "So, you're sanctioning me to get her drunk? And then find out what she did to Sean? And then convince her to patch things up with her daughter? And then to join the Federation?"

Lance chuckled, getting up. "Just intel on Sean would be good to begin with. One step at a time, eh?"

Barb breathed heavily through her nose, clearly amused.

"Okay, I'll get onto the research and see what I can do. Wanna let me know when she gets here?" she suggested getting up and wandering back across the office.

"Sure thing. Thanks, Barb."

"Any time," she replied. "Frank's lack of organization was driving me nuts. I'm glad of the break." She checked the picture on the wall one last time before waving and heading out of the office.

Lance watched her, smiling to himself and shaking his head. *Good ol' Barb,* he thought before turning his attention back to work.

CHAPTER SIX

<u>Glom Space station, Kirox Quadrant</u>

Ronnie Matherson was a loser.

But when he was brought into the family by his uncle, there were those who thought that maybe it would be the making of him. After all, how hard would it be to just show up, look tough, and deliver the odd message now and again?

Right now, Ronnie wished that he'd stuck to the original tasks that his employer had assigned him. Bill always said that thinking wasn't his strong suit.

Ronnie turned sharply right and headed down a passage between two establishments. His eyes scanned for somewhere to hide. An air vent. A cupboard. A garbage chute.

Anything to escape the advancing cyborg that was hot on his trail.

Karina was pretty. But not pretty enough to die for. No amount of money she had paid him was worth this.

He thought it was going to be easy. Easy money and easy pride. A job: one he could finally pull off on his own.

Breathing hard, his eyes darted from shadow to shadow, looking for a hiding place that might save him. The chatter of the main station thoroughfare behind him fell like a curtain, offering him a false sense of protection from advancing doom.

He found a recess in the wall behind a panel. It was narrow, but it was going to have to do. Darting over to it like a tiny space rat, he pulled himself round, clumsily catching the back of his hand against the sharp edge of the panel. He pressed himself up against the side of the next building and tried to slow his breathing. He felt beads of sweat dripping from his head and down his neck and face. He felt like he'd been running for hours.

It was likely only a few minutes, though. That, he knew. And cyborgs don't get tired.

He felt his own body heat warming the air around him now he was stationary. He hated himself. He hated how he got himself into these messes. And he hated that this time, out on his own, with no one from the family to mop up his mess, he was going to die.

Peering from behind the panel, he saw the silhouette of his pursuer appearing in the alley.

Fuck, fuck, fuck, he cursed silently. *It wasn't fair.*

He tried to hold back his whimpering. It was only a matter of moments before he was going to be found. His eyes welled with tears of terror and sadness.

The cyborg started moving toward him, getting closer and closer with each step.

No way was he getting out of this.

"I see you, dumbass," the man called. His voice was tough. Tougher than any of the hard asses he'd ever worked for. Like Federation-tough.

Ronnie accidentally let out a whimper.

The voice called him again. "Come out of there, space rat, and I might let you live."

Ronnie's face clenched up in anguish. He had never been so afraid in his worthless life.

"*Come out!*" The man ordered again, making Ronnie jump out of his skin.

As if his legs had grown a will of their own, or at least an obedience to his executioner, they marched him out from behind the panel of atmospheric controls.

"Good," the cyborg said with an undertone of menace. "Now, we're going to go right back to that restaurant, and you and Karina are going to explain to me *exactly* why she told you you were shooting 'too close'."

Ronnie's face dropped. Then he realized that he had automatically put his hands up. He started lowering them before he realized the threat hadn't passed. He quickly put them back up.

"Come, *now*," Sean ordered, striding back out of the artificial alleyway.

Knowing he had neither the balls, firepower, nor speed to do anything else, Ronnie resigned himself to his fate and followed the all-powerful cyborg promptly.

The unlikely pair wove their way back through the corridors they had given chase down just minutes before.

The cyborg never once checked behind him to make sure that Ronnie was following.

Probably got some kind of biometric lock on me, Ronnie thought to himself dejectedly.

It took some minutes to return to the restaurant, but as they approached, they saw two rather large, enhanced men carrying Karina.

"Oi!" Sean shouted out to them. People in the crowd looked at him. Before Ronnie understood what was happening, Sean was on the move. "Move and I'll find you and kill you," he shouted back to Ronnie. Ronnie froze on the spot.

Sean barged his way through the people, trying to get to the men carrying Karina. "Oi!" he shouted.

One of the men took Karina over both shoulders now, and the other one turned, pointing a weapon at Sean.

Sean could see, even from this distance, that Karina was out cold. Her body hung limply, but Sean refused to believe she could be dead. It wouldn't make sense to carry a dead body like that.

The second man fired a warning shot just above the crowd. There were screams as shoppers and diners scattered like ants, suddenly aware of the danger.

Sean lunged to the side of the street, finding cover behind a raised walkway. Immediately though, he started advancing again.

He peeked up over the edge of the raised platform that was used by the restaurants as a patio. He could see the two goons hurrying away: one with the girl, the other with a pistol sweeping their path behind them, fending off any attacks.

Sean drew his weapon and scuttled after them, keeping low and out of sight.

He watched as they disappeared around the corner, and then ran as hard as he could through the crowd of frightened punters who still hadn't managed to get out of the way. Turning the corner, he saw them running in extended gait: something only cyborgs could do with their enhanced muscles and reflexes. He pounded down the corridor after them, pushing his own reflexes and power into extended mode.

Thump thump thump thump...

He felt the vibration of the station structure through his joints as he ran, weapon held up ready to fire as soon as he got a clear shot.

The pair disappeared around the next corner.

Thump thump thump thump...

It would have taken a normal human at least three times as long to cover this distance. His brain turned to figuring out where they might be going. On a station such as this, there were going to be very few places they could hide. Though weapons were allowed, they didn't look like they were packing more than a pistol or two, and they were heading to the outer reach of the station, not inwards.

That means they're going for the docks, he decided. He needed to reach them before they got her onto a shuttle. Otherwise, they'd be gone forever.

His mind flicked through the possibility of going back to Scamp. But Scamp was on the other side of the station, back the other way. With the number of ships coming and going, there was no way he'd be able to find the right one once they got spaceborne.

He pushed harder, trying to keep up. He slowed a tad just to take the corner. He placed his feet carefully, so as not to slip, his keen gaze assessing the speed and positioning faster than everything was happening. He raised his gaze as he rounded the corner. His body reacted before his brain had processed what was happening. One of the cyborgs was right there, pointing his gun down the corridor, poised and waiting for Sean to appear.

BANG.

BANG bang bang.

Sean felt himself losing his footing. Then, his head was whipped violently to the side, and he felt himself change direction.

He was floating through the air, and then, nothing.

Nothingness lasted a little while until gradually, he became aware of the nothingness.

Then, he felt his head throbbing. He went to move and felt cold concrete beneath him. He managed to lift his head, trying to open his eyes against the light. Squinting and aching, he felt like he had been hit by a train.

Eventually, he realized what had happened and brought himself up to a sitting position. Dragging himself, aching, up against the side of the tunnel he had been running through, he checked himself for injury. He looked down at his chest. There was a laser burn the size of a billiard ball in the top layers of his atmosuit.

Thank fuck for Federation-issue suits, he thought to himself, delicately prodding his fingers into the holes in the carbon-fiber layers beneath.

He tried to take a deep breath but winced. It may have stopped the round, but his body still had to dissipate the momentum. And momentum burned like a motherfucker.

Still in pain, he leaned forward over his legs and started to haul himself up. There was no telling how long he'd been out, but one thing was certain: whoever those guys were, they had Karina, and by now, they were long gone.

He looked up the corridor, briefly wondering if he should carry on anyway and try and narrow down who had been there.

Then he remembered the space rat he had been about to haul into questioning. He turned back the way he came and started limping down the corridors as fast as his cyborg ass would carry him.

Maybe he'd give Karina's flunky a chance to redeem himself, after all.

Sean was moving a little more naturally by the time he arrived back in the main part of the station. His pain modulators had kicked in, and repair had already begun on the bruising in his chest. He'd also found a lump on his head where he must have hit it during his fall. That was the biggest danger of being able to move so fast. It hurt like hell when you were forced to stop quickly.

Things had started to return to normal already. Station security were doing their thing, cordoning of the area and milling around, presumably talking to witnesses. Sean made his way up to the scene, careful to maintain a large enough distance so that he didn't look too curious. His eyes scanned the area, picking up all the minute details that might be relevant later. Nothing caught his attention, though.

He passed by, leaving the scene behind him, his eyes now scanning for Karina's contact. If anyone was going to be able to tell him what the fuck was going on, it was going to be him.

Sean chuckled to himself as he approached the spot where he had told the reprobate to stay put. Part of him thought he might do it just because he was scared and stupid. Part of him was disappointed that he hadn't. It would have amused him. He kept his eyes peeled as he walked, retracing his step, trying to figure out where his mark might have gone.

If the lackey was cooperating, he'd stay nearby. If not, he'd be long gone. Sean decided to assume for now that he'd be somewhere within eye shot so that when Sean returned—

A movement caught his eye over to his right. Just outside the shadows of a crevice between two faux-fronted buildings, he caught sight of the sweaty, inept human he had been chasing. Seeing Sean, the scrawny human nodded and then stepped back into the shadows.

Sean crossed the walkway and headed over to meet him.

"Good decision," he grunted as he approached the alley.

Ronnie looked up at him. "I got out of the way, though. Station security turned up."

Sean nodded. "Fine. Okay, now you're going to start from the beginning and tell me exactly what is going on."

The human swallowed. "Okay," he agreed.

Minutes later, Ronnie had introduced himself and told Sean the story so far. Sean hadn't needed to resort to any form of violence, to his mild disappointment.

"So, Karina hired you to lay down fire and lure me in. But that doesn't explain who those assholes were who took her."

Ronnie wrung his hands nervously. "I dunno who they are. I thought it might have been part of her plan."

Sean pursed his lips. "It could be. But I don't want to take that chance. Who might they be?"

"What do you mean? I just told you I have no idea who they are."

Sean stepped forward menacingly.

Ronnie flinched. "I dunno. I swear. I've never seen them before!"

Sean looked down at him sternly. *Maybe violence isn't out of the question,* he mused to himself.

"Look," he said out loud, "the odds are, if you know Karina in this sector of space, you're dodgy. I'd bet my Federation pension on it. So, I'll ask you again. Given who the big bad is in this sector, who is it likely to be?"

"Erm, well, if I had a gun to my head and I had to guess," Ronnie said slowly, perspiring again. Sean raised his eyebrows, reacting to the gun to his head comment. "I'd say maybe the family," Ronnie finished hastily. He gulped.

"Which family?" Sean pressed, his agitation now showing.

"The Calzones."

Sean's complexion turned gray. He lost his train of thought for a moment. "Okay," he said, floundering a little. "Lemme guess, you work for the family."

His tone made it a statement.

"How do you know?" Ronnie asked, staggering back half a step to restore some space between them.

Sean shook his head. "Sorry to tell you this, kid, but you're a walking cliche."

Ronnie's eyebrows knotted. "Oh. I dunno what that means."

"Never mind. It's a good thing today."

"Why's that?"

"Because," Sean explained, "it means that you're going to be able to help me."

Ronnie was still flummoxed. "How?"

Sean was regaining his posture, though. "Since you work for the people who are likely holding Karina, you can get me into where Karina is being taken."

Ronnie started backing up, stumbling in the darkness of the alley. "No. No way. Not if she's going where I think she's going."

Sean stepped forward again. "You will. Or I'll kill you where you stand."

Petrified again, Ronnie froze on the spot. Sean watched as the fear subsided and turned to utter dismay. His shoulders slumped. "Well, I guess I don't have a choice."

"Good," Sean grunted, his mood not changed even a little by Ronnie's agreement. "Now that that's arranged, let's go take a look at your ship. See what we're dealing with."

Sean marched Ronnie to check Ronnie's ship. Satisfied it was spacefaring and agile enough, he then frog-marched him back to the dock where he had left Scamp.

"Climb on," he said, nodding toward the invisible staircase.

Ronnie looked at him in confusion. "I, erm… need to wait for the stair lift or something."

Sean chuckled to himself. He didn't have time to drag this out. He pushed past Ronnie and started climbing. Ronnie watched in awe and then scrambled up after him.

"Don't touch anything. Don't ask any questions. I need to talk to my computer and then we're leaving."

Sean showed Ronnie into the kitchen of *The Scamp Princess* and left him there while he went to talk with Scamp in the cockpit.

Aboard *The Scamp Princess*, docked at Glom Space station, Kirox Quadrant

Sean sat in silence for a few moments in the cockpit. Thinking. Contemplating.

"Scamp?"

"Yes, Sean?"

"I'm going to have to take another ride to where Karina is."

"Why?"

"Because if I show up in *The Scamp Princess,* they're gonna see me coming, and they'll hurt Karina."

"I see."

"I need you to wait here for me."

"Sean?"

"Yes?"

"Is it dangerous?"

"Nah. It'll be a walk in the park."

"Only, if it's dangerous, we should talk about what I should do if you don't come back. My programming is to return to the Federation after twenty-four hours, unmanned."

There was silence for a few moments.

"Can we override your programming?" Sean asked.

"Only if it is mission critical."

Sean thought a while longer. "Well, how about this: you wait for me here for three days. If I don't come back, then you return to Molly so that she can complete the mission?"

"What mission?"

"That's above your pay grade, Scamp."

"You're saying that so I have to override the twenty-four-hour window."

"Maybe I am. But either way, you have to do it, right?"

"You are correct."

"Good." Sean pushed himself up out of the pilot's chair and winced.

"Are you damaged Sean?"

"Nothing a good night's sleep won't fix."

"I don't think you should be trying to do whatever you're doing on your own."

"I have no choice, Scamp." Sean laid his hand gently on the top of the console. "You've been a good friend, Scamp. Thank you for everything."

And then he strode out of the cockpit.

"Why did that feel like a goodbye?" Scamp muttered to the empty room.

Sean poked his head into the kitchen. "Alright, Ronnie. Time to move."

Ronnie hadn't had time to poke around and was still sitting quietly at the table. He jumped up and followed Sean quickly out of the kitchen and then through the passageway back out of the side door with the invisible steps.

He hesitated as his foot hit something firm that he couldn't see. And then he trotted down after his new master.

Sean didn't even look back. When the two were off the staircase, Ronnie could hear some kind of machinery moving, and then the door closed, and the locks slid mechanically into place.

He glanced back briefly and almost ran into a maintenance cart on the dock. Flustered, he turned his attention just to following Sean and then jogged to catch up to him.

The pair arrived back at Ronnie's ship in no time. Sean obviously had a good memory. Or he knew the station. Ronnie dared not ask which. He seemed even more agitated than before.

"Okay," Sean gruffed, climbing on board. "Let's get her out of here as fast as possible."

Ronnie obeyed quietly, full of dread for what Sean was about to make him do.

C H A P T E R   S E V E N

<u>Unknown location, somewhere in Kirox Quadrant</u>

Karina came to in a cold room. She moved her head, twisting to see where she was. She was lying on some kind of bench. She swung her legs around to sit up and felt a chain drag. Opening her eyes, she realized where she was. And she didn't like it.

Metal bars made up one wall. Cold gray stone made up the other three. She was chained by one ankle to a bolt in the wall by the bench she was lying on.

Shit.

"Guard!" she shouted. No response. "Guaaaaaaaaaard!" she screamed again.

No one came.

She slumped back against the wall, then curled her legs up to her chest. She knew how this went, and she could end up being here a while.

She sat in the half light, thinking.

If only she had told Mrs. Bates "no," she wouldn't be here now. Or she could have just come clean to Sean. She didn't have to lure him out here. Or get that Ronnie kid to make things look realistic. And how the hell did these goons find her?

Her mind reeled, searching for understanding.

Odds were, they'd killed Sean right there on the station. So that was her fault.

She felt her insides implode with guilt. *Her life was once again well and truly fucked. Only this time, there was no Sean Royale to pick up the pieces.*

She rested her head back against the cold wall. *Fuck.*

Footsteps. There were footsteps coming from the other end of the corridor. That meant someone probably wanted to talk to her. A guard appeared. "Okay, princess. You're up."

The guard didn't wear a uniform. None of them did in this group. That was the family way. They were paid as employees but expected to act as... well, family. Complete loyalty was demanded. And assumed. The alternative is... well, death.

The man was human but enhanced. Karina couldn't be sure that he was one of the goons that got the jump on her. They all looked the same out here, with their over-beefed muscles and worn atmosuits.

It didn't matter anyway. She always knew that one day she would probably have to face the music.

The guard put her in arm braces and then undid the chain on her ankle. "Move," he grunted, pushing her toward the open door.

"You didn't bring any backup to fetch me?" she asked, trying to provoke him for no other reason than she was annoyed and wanted to take it out on someone.

"Didn't need it, sweetheart. Nothing much you can do. Nowhere to run." He grabbed her upper arm roughly and pushed her ahead of him down the corridor, toward the lighted building beyond.

The flunky led Karina up through a series of walkways and corridors and into a mag-lev elevator. Karina recognized it, but it had been a long time since she was last here, and there were certain things that had changed. She wouldn't like to have to navigate her way out of this place under duress.

But then, this didn't seem to be a day where she was going to get everything she wanted.

Eventually, the cyborg brought her to a door. He knocked. A gruff voice answered from the other side. The flunky hit the "open door" button and shoved her inside.

The decor was warm and expensive. Carpets. Curtains. All the trappings of an executive suite on a trading outpost. A trading outpost in a corner of the galaxy she would rather have never visited again.

The man who was in command of everything on the outpost stood looking out of the window, out into space and the dock activity on the other side of the station.

"Karina," he cooed, without turning around. "Nice of you to join me."

Karina scowled and tugged herself away from the cyborg that was escorting her. "Yeah. The pleasure is all yours, Dad."

Don Calzone turned around to look at his daughter. "Is that all you have to say to your Papa after all these years?"

Karina glared at him. "What can I say? I'm not the sentimental type."

The Don's expression turned serious. "Me neither," he shared. "I should kill you where you stand."

Karina raised her chin defiantly. "Fine. Do it. I'd much rather die than end up locked in a cage in this shithole."

The Don's eyes flared, and his complexion turned red with fury. "How dare you talk to me like that?"

"How dare you have me put in your shitty dungeon like that?" Her demeanor shifted. Since leaving this place, she had learned to hold herself in a certain way. A way that wouldn't draw attention. A way that would allow her to look humble and deferent. But now, back under the same oppressive conditions, she felt her old ways coming back. Her back straightened, and her shoulders went back, ready to assert her authority, even to her father, the local crime lord.

"Well, you are behaving like the enemy!" he spat in fury, clearly unaccustomed to anyone challenging him since her departure.

"That's what happens when you treat people like the enemy!"

"I did everything for you," he protested, his anger spilling out into a lecture she had heard a million times. "I educated you. I taught you our ways. I prepared you to take over the family business."

She didn't miss a beat in her response. "I didn't want to take over the goddam business. I hate what you do!"

Vito wasn't going to be beaten. He slammed his hand on his desk. "There's a fine line between love and hate. You would have grown to love it. Just like I did. And my Papa before me." His anger was falling away as he ranted, clearly showing he no longer had the energy he once did. He sat down at his desk, a look of exhaustion on his drawn face.

"I hated you for the longest time," he added more quietly. "But then, I thought you'd died. I had no idea you just betrayed me."

He picked a laser gun up off his desk, his energy renewed. He got up and walked toward her with it. "I should blow your head off right now, though. Send a message to all those who might cross me!"

Karina maintained her posture. "I'd be surprised if you need me to send a message. From what I remember, you were always pulling shit like that, just in case someone, somewhere might undermine your authority."

"Well, it worked!"

"It's pathetic," she spat venomously.

The Don's fight disappeared from him, and his shoulders slumped as if the plug had been pulled out of a blown up balloon. "Karina..." he started, his voice hesitant now.

"No, don't 'Karina' me, Dad. You dragged me out here. I was in the middle of something. What do you want?"

The Don sighed. "I want… I want my daughter back."

He paused.

Karina waited.

"All this time, I thought you were dead. I wanted to *kill* you for not being more careful. And then, *then*, I find out that you're alive. And not only are you alive, but that you left with that spy!"

"He wasn't a spy." She paused, the cogs turning behind her eyes. "How did you know I left with him?"

Calzone shrugged, the fight fully left him now. "I didn't. Until you just confirmed it. Then… there were rumors you were still alive."

"Well, whatever," she grunted, looking pointedly at the arm cuffs. "It's not important now."

The Don sighed.

"So, what's your move now, Dad?" she asked, emphasizing the word "Dad." "You bring me up here to torture me with your shit? And then you're going to kill me?" Years of pain tainted the timbre of her voice.

"No," the old man confessed. "I'm not going to kill you. I thought I would," he qualified quickly, his ego rising. "But over the years, I've come to realize that there is nothing like family. You're my daughter. And despite what you've done in the past to hurt me, I want you to come home."

"That's very big of you," she shot back sarcastically. "Not going to happen. I'll take the bullet, thanks."

"But Karina, don't you see? I'm extending an olive branch. I want us to be together again. To be happy."

She shook her head, her chin still held out obstinately. "No way I can be happy with you around. You're a tyrant."

"I'm not!"

Something on his desk buzzed, pulling his attention. Karina

struggled to see if she could get free from the braces, without any luck.

Calzone hit his ear. "Yes?"

Someone on the other end of the line was telling him something. Suddenly, his eyes shot back to Karina. "Ah. I see. Yes, throw him in the dungeon for now. I'll talk to him later."

He hit the implant behind his ear again. "Seems we have company."

Docking Bay, Bronislovas Trading Outpost, Kirox Quadrant

Ronnie's beaten-up shuttle clunked into place in the docking bay. "You know, if we turn back now, we may stand a chance..." Ronnie suggested, his voice wobbling with stress.

Sean shook his head. "We're going in." He flicked a few switches, locking the ship in the dock so that the door switches would go live. "You stay here if you want, but this ship needs to be here when I get back. It's our only escape."

Ronnie nodded. "And your plan is to just walk in there?"

Sean was up and out of his seat, heading for the door. "Something tells me it will be easy to walk in there."

The side door opened to reveal a small welcome party of family goons standing just inside the docking bay door. Ronnie took one look and scuttled back into the ship to hide. Sean, however, stepped down the stepladder as casually as if he were showing up to a friend's place.

"Hello, fellas," he called out to them. He noticed that one had a black eye. "Nice shiner. Where'd ya get that? Not from a girl by any chance?"

The cyborg glared back at him while two of the others moved forward. Sean put his hands in the air. "It's all right, fellas. I want to be here. Take me to your leader." He smirked to himself.

The two on either side of him put him into an arm brace, restraining his hands in front of him.

With a hint of humor and a big dose of complacency, he sidled up to one of them and, in a low voice, started talking to him. "Tell me, you haven't seen a girl around here. Average build. About yay tall." He held his hands up, despite the arm brace holding them together at the wrist. "Goes by the name of Karina? Packs a mean left hook?"

The flunky's pupil dilation showed signs of recognition, but he said nothing. He took one of Sean's arms, and another guy with guns on both legs took his other. Both had strong grips, and judging by the strength of them, Sean guessed they had some enhanced cyborg capabilities.

He heard a scuffle behind him and one of the muscle heads talking to Ronnie. They must have pulled him from the ship. "Boss will be very interested to see you," he heard as he was pushed out of the docking bay door. "You're in big trouble."

The same voice called after them. "I'll let him know about both of them." The man on his left grunted something in acknowledgment, and they continued on their way.

Sean tried to turn back to see, but the third guy behind him pushed him forward again and blocked his view.

His sheer strength wasn't going to get him out of this one. He was going to have to rely on something he knew from previous experience these guys wouldn't have: wits.

Compliantly, he allowed himself to be led through the corridors from the docking bay, deeper and deeper into the station.

From the looks of the people around, this was a trading outpost. Humans and a host of other humanoid races passed by with crates and carts. Some also passed by with nothing but their digital holos, which would allow them to trade and communicate and move funds at the flick of a finger. They were dressed for comfort and show. Not for battle or practicalities.

And yet, no one batted a scaly eyelid at the fact that he was being restrained and moved through the station by two un-uniformed meatheads.

Sean wracked his brains to the last time he was here. The family certainly had all the control they needed back then. Maybe their operations weren't even covert now. Could that be? That their dodgy dealings were out in the open?

He continued absorbing all the intel he could on the way, remembering each twist and turn so he could make his way back once he found Karina.

If he could find Karina.

The fact that she was taken and not killed on the spot suggested she was wanted alive, at least. But for how long? Not even Ronnie had been able to tell him that.

Ronnie had been taken in another direction, also in cuffs. He was on his own. And finding Karina on this trading outpost was going to be like trying to find a needle in a haystack.

Where's a friendly AI when you need one? he mused to himself dryly.

Calzone's office, Bronislovas Trading Outpost, Kirox Quadrant

The Don pressed his lips together. "You might be interested to know that it looks like your spy friend has come to save you," he announced.

A tiny smile played across Karina's lips.

Her father spotted it. "Ahh, so that makes you happy? That's the first time I've seen you smile since you came back!"

Karina wanted to protest that she wasn't back but bit her tongue.

He rocked gently in his chair. "Tell me, is this the same man who took you away from me?" She could see a new wave of anger boiling up in him.

Karina nodded her head. "Yes. He saved me from you."

He deflated again, crushed. "*Saved* you from me? What are you talking about?"

Karina resisted the urge to roll her eyes. She'd been dealing with her father's ridiculous ego all her life. Explaining logic or the real world to him had never had any positive effect. If anything, it only tended to push him to dig his heels in even more. "You were going to have me killed, remember? For being insolent or something."

He looked off into the distance, searching for the distant memory. "Yes… you may be right. I was a lot more… volatile back then. But things are different now. It used to be that we were fighting tooth and nail with the Bertolis just to survive. But now… now we're the big man!" He sounded proud.

Karina tempered her natural response to his pride. "So, you're not going to kill me anymore?" She doubted very much he would catch the sarcasm in her voice.

"Kill you? No, my daughter. I've missed you… it turns out."

Karina rolled her eyes.

"I'm glad you're alive," he continued. "And though I'd like to kill you for deserting me like that… no. It's all water under the bridge. I'm going to start being a better father to you."

"Really," she responded flatly.

There was no way he could miss the sarcasm there.

"Yes. Don't you see? If I was the same man, you'd still be in chains in the dungeon."

Clearly, sarcasm is forever lost on him, she noted to herself. *Like emotional intelligence.*

"Oh yeah?" she pressed out loud. "And where did you put my friend?"

Though he was missing her points, he didn't miss a beat in his response. "In the dungeon, of course."

Karina shook her head. "So, you haven't changed."

"I have. I want you to be happy." He sat down on the sofa near where she stood and patted the seat next to him. "So, tell me, Karina Calzone. What would make you happy?"

Karina wandered around the room, looking at the various

artifacts his wealth and power had acquired for him. This room wasn't part of his operation fifteen years ago. "It would make me happy for you to let me and my friend go," she suggested, her gaze wandering, taking in any piece of information that might help her predicament.

"My daughter," he said. "You're free to go whenever you want."

"And my friend?"

"No," he said firmly. "He helped you escape."

Karina's hands were up at her face in frustration. She tugged at her hair, peeking out from behind her cuffs. This man had always lacked in the brain cell department. Luckily, she had inherited her mother's intellect.

"Okay, Papa, let me go back to the dungeon. I'd like to be with my friend."

"Very well," he replied childishly. He moved his finger for the guards to take her. Then he stopped.

"Hang on," he said, stopping the guard with another move of his finger. "This 'friend' makes you happy?"

"Yes, Papa."

"Is he handsome?"

Karina frowned and screwed up her lips, trying to come to terms with the bizarre question. "I guess."

"Is he a gay?"

Karina shook her head, shocked. "Erm. No. I don't think he's *gay*, Papa."

"Well, then it's settled. You and he will be married." He jumped up, grinning and excited. He walked over to her and held her cheeks in his thumbs. "My little girl is getting married!"

Karina's mouth dropped open, and she pulled away from him. "You've got to be fucking kidding me. That's the leap you make? Dungeon to marriage?"

The demented old man shrugged. "It's quite simple, as I see it. This man—"

"Sean," Karina interjected.

He began again. "I want my baby to be happy. Sean makes you happy. You will marry Sean." He pinched her cheeks and wiggled them like she was a doll or a dog. "Simple."

Karina managed to pull away and started to protest the madness.

Calzone barely heard her. "It will be a marriage for the sector to remember. Harry!" He called over the guard that, seconds before, had been about to take Karina back to the dungeon. "Send Ricardo in here. We must start making arrangements immediately. I think we should hold it at the station church. This Saturday. It will be a wonderful event. The envy of every fairytale princess."

Don Calzone continued to prattle. Karina rubbed her cheeks where he'd been pinching them and then wiped her face with her hands again in frustration.

"I think I preferred it better when you were just going to throw me in the dungeon," she muttered.

"Oh, that can be arranged," he shot back, his voice suddenly cruel. He motioned for her to be taken. "Take her back… until she realizes I just want what's best for her."

His voice softened again, and the optimistic excitement of a new project returned. "Hurry up and come around to this," he told her, a finger on her chin. "There's so much planning to do, and it would be more fun if you were up here helping me with it!"

Then, he giggled like a lunatic and sat behind his desk as his entourage came in and started the busy work of planning her wedding.

CHAPTER EIGHT

<u>**Dungeon, Calzone's offices, Bronislovas Trading Outpost, Kirox Quadrant**</u>

Her head still spinning, Karina allowed herself to be led back to her cell in the so-called dungeon.

As she and her guard approached the corridor, it suddenly dawned on her that she was probably about to see Sean. After all these years, and having just pulled the most stupid stunt of her whole existence, she was going to have to face him.

She felt the anxiety rising up in her chest. She felt embarrassed. And stupid. And wished there were some way to make everything right again, before she had to face him.

But then, this wasn't a day where she was getting anything she wanted.

The guard pushed her forward. "Hurry up," he grunted. "Haven't got all day."

Movement caught her eye in the cell to her right. She was frog-marched straight past it and back into the one she had been in before. She didn't dare turn around to look. There was no doubt the person in there had seen her, though. She could hear the movement as he reacted.

The guard clamped the ankle restraint around her again and tugged at it. Satisfied it was secure, he turned and left, clanking the cell gate behind him and then reactivating whatever godforsaken security field they had installed with a swipe on the panel on the far wall as he left.

"Are you having as bad a day as I am?" a voice asked from the next cell. It was male and deep. She'd recognize it anywhere.

"Sean Royale," she said slowly, wondering where the hell this conversation could possibly go. "As I live and breathe."

There was a pause. "Well, let's hope we can keep that living and breathing thing going. Word on the street is that folks who end up in here don't end up doing much of that after a while."

Karina chuckled lightly. "It's good to hear your voice, Royale."

"Yours, too."

There was another awkward silence.

Sean spoke again. "Don't suppose you have any ideas on how to get out of here?"

"I have a few," she confessed. "None that you'd like, though."

"Oh yeah? Why's that?"

"Because just like any man, I think you value your freedom, and ironically, that's going to be the one thing you'll have to give up…"

"You're kidding me?" Karina could hear Sean pacing in the next cell. "You're saying that not only did you lure me here under false and very dangerous pretenses, but that now our only way out of this is to go along with your father's ridiculous idea for winning his daughter back."

Karina was tired of talking. It had taken a while to explain everything to Sean, and if she were honest, it was a relief to hear him talking. He'd been silent throughout the whole explanation.

Now he ranted. "I can't begin to fathom what possessed you

to go down this route in the first place. Why didn't you just come to me? Tell me what she was doing?"

Karina sighed. "I thought that if I did this one thing, then she'd truly leave me alone. For good."

Sean sighed heavily. "From what I've heard about her, that woman ain't one for letting things go. I mean, case in point. She sends you to ensnare me!"

Karina sighed and covered her face with her hands again. "I know. I'm sorry!"

"I also can't believe this guy is your father," he huffed. The pacing continued. "Had I known that..."

"What? What would you have done? Left me here to rot?"

Sean sighed again. "I... I don't know. Probably not." The pacing stopped. His voice dropped. "I just wish I'd known."

Karina rolled her eyes, lying on her back in the next cell. "Well, I wished I had a pony growing up, but we both know that all I got was the normal things a mob princess got: death and the constant threat of death."

"Well, moping around won't help us. If the only way out of this is to agree to his terms, then I guess that's what we need to do."

Karina was silent.

"Karina? You still there?"

"Of course I am. No. Wait. I just popped out for a mochaccino."

"Sarcasm never suited you."

"Well, neither does having my freedoms taken away from me."

"Touché," he said. "So, erm, before we agree to do this... tell me... you've kept yourself in shape, right?"

Karina's blood started to boil. "You've got to be fucking kidding me?" She kicked up off the bench. "I swear, Sean Royale, I wouldn't marry you if you were the last man in the fucking galaxy. Or if our lives depended on it. And as for me keeping myself in shape, get your ass in here and I'd show you how goddamn in shape I am when I rip you a new one. And another thing—"

Chuckling emanated from Sean's cell.

Karina stopped, her need to put a fist through something somewhat tempered by only having metal bars and stone walls around. "What's so fucking funny?"

"Nothing. I just thought I should get that one in before they released us."

"You what?"

"Just that. It was too good of an opportunity to miss."

"You're just fucking with me?" she asked.

"Erm, yeah." He paused. "Mostly."

Karina continued to fume. It was her turn to pace. "Sean Royale, I swear the minute we're out of this, I'm going to—"

Just then, there were footsteps coming down the corridor.

Sean whispered across to her. "Let's just go along with it. Tell them you're ready to speak to your father and get us out of this hellhole."

The flunky arrived back at the bars. "Your father sent me down to see if you've made your mind up about cooperating yet."

Karina stood quietly in the middle of the room, her hands clasped in front of her and her eyes lowered to the floor. "I have. And he's right. Sean and I should get married."

Aboard _The Empress_, Kirox Quadrant

Molly fidgeted in frustration. It wasn't just on account of all the waiting around, but from all the emotions she was trying to keep a lid on, too. She thought about going and sitting somewhere to meditate. She knew that would be the right move. Or at least what Arlene would recommend.

She just felt defiant, though. Joel had fallen asleep again, and Jack and Pieter were playing some kind of game that was keeping them engrossed. She stood up, stretching her legs and back as best she could in the cramped area. Then quietly, she slipped over Joel's outstretched legs, out into the main walkway, and up to the corridor that led to the cockpit.

She appeared in the cockpit next to Brock, who seemed to be working hard at the console panel.

"Everything okay?" she asked.

Brock jumped, letting out a small falsetto whoop of surprise. Laughing from his belly, he turned to her. "My ancestors, guuuu-url! Don't go sneaking up on people like that!"

He had his hand on his chest as if trying to calm his heart down. Crash turned to see what all the fuss was about, and a tiny smile appeared on his lips when he saw Brock's expression.

"So?" Molly pressed, ignoring the dramedy. "Where are we?"

Crash eyed her playfully. "What you mean to ask is: why is this taking so damn long, don't you?"

Molly nodded sheepishly. "Well… yeah. But I didn't want you to think I was on your case. You my boyzzzz." She punched Brock's arm gently, winning him over in a heartbeat.

"Yeah, yeah," he continued. "It's a fair question." He jerked his thumb over in Crash's direction. "Mister Grumpy over there has been asking me the same question… over and over."

Crash shrugged and turned back to his controls. Molly found it hard to imagine Crash saying more than he physically needed to.

Brock pulled up a screen to show Molly what was going on. "You see, we need to retrace Scamp's steps, but because we've jumped, we have no universal coordinates we can retrace. We're having to track it in loci."

Molly nodded. "Oh, I see. So, it's like we do two steps this way and five steps that way… rather than go straight to point X."

"You got it," Brock confirmed. "So… here we are in the middle of fricking nowhere, where Sean stayed for five minutes at a standstill."

Molly frowned. "Do we know why?"

Brock shook his head.

"Can we get eyes on outside?" she asked.

Crash hit a button and obligingly brought the front screen up to show them what was outside.

Everything was dark and blank.

Molly shuddered.

"You okay, hon?" Brock asked.

She wrapped her arms around herself. "Yeah. I just got a chill."

Brock narrowed his eyes. "Like a cold chill? Or a realm-jumping chill?"

Molly dropped her eyes again and shuffled her feet. "I dunno. I just thought of Sean being here and wondered where he could be now… and I just got this wash of dread through me. Like he's in a really bad place." She shook her head. "Ignore me. Wild imagination."

Brock watched her carefully. "No, no. I think there is something to this. I haven't forgotten the stories of those other missions where Sean was on that planet, and you were running from the guards and could feel them coming." He paused, his face deadly serious now. "Your realm stuff saved their lives."

Molly continued to study the toes of her boots. "Well… anyway. We just need to get to Sean and get him home."

Brock nodded. "Agreed." He poked the screen he was working on. "Anyway, it looks like he moved on from here pretty quickly. Ancestors know what he was doing out here. There's a slight ion trail, like there was a small explosion, but Scamp was undamaged, so it probably wasn't anything significant. We've got one more jump to do."

Molly bobbed her head, placing a hand on Brock's shoulder. "Okay. I'll leave you to get us there and get the others ready to move." She started heading out of the cockpit.

Brock smiled. "Okay. And Molly?"

She turned back. "Yeah?"

"It's going to be okay. Sean is a tough cookie, and we're going to find him."

She grinned, snapping into her best impression of how she imagined Bethany Anne might have been when she was on missions. "Yeah… and I'll kick his ass myself when I get my hands on him!"

Brock was oblivious to the influence but laughed at her sudden display of chutzpah. "I'm sure he'll be looking forward to that, too," he muttered humorously as he plotted the coordinates for Emma and Crash to implement.

Bronislovas Trading Outpost, Kirox Quadrant

Sean woke up shivering. He opened his eyes and blearily looked around the cold cell.

No change there then, he figured.

Immediately, the first thoughts in his mind were of Karina.

"Karina?" he hissed urgently. *"Karina?"*

"What?" Her voice was laced with irritation.

"Are you there?"

As soon as the words had left his mouth, he could almost feel her eyes rolling in her head through the stone wall that separated them.

"No numb nuts, I'm upstairs eating fucking caviar."

He sat up. "Are we alone?"

"I dunno," she responded, her voice softening. "I guess."

He got up and shuffled to the bars, listening carefully for any other signs of life. He glanced down at his handcuffs. He twisted his hands over and found a catch to release them.

They dropped and clanked noisily against the stone floor.

"What was that?" Karina hissed, agitated they were going to draw attention.

Sean glanced down at the cuffs on the floor and his now naked wrists. "I've managed to get out of my handcuffs."

"How the hell did you manage that?"

"I don't know. It just occurred to me I knew how to hack them. There's a switch on the underneath side."

He heard Karina jingling hers. "Shit, I can't reach it," she grunted.

He noticed a small rod of metal and immediately thought to use it as a lock pick. He picked it up and poked it around inside the lock.

"It's okay," Sean whispered back. "Hang tight. I'm just picking this door lock."

Karina huffed, and the sound of movement from her side of the wall stopped. "How on Earth can you pick the lock?"

Sean shrugged, even though she couldn't see him. "I'm not sure," he confessed. "But… it's totally pick-able."

A moment later, it clicked, and the lock snapped open. He pushed against the cage door, and it swung open on its hinges.

"Holy shit, Batman! You've managed it!" Karina sounded impressed.

"Yeah, shh. We don't want to draw any attention." He slipped quietly out of the cage and replaced the door so that it didn't bang. Skillfully and quickly, he started working on the lock on Karina's cage. The lock yielded in seconds, and Sean pulled at the door, opening it with a slight bow and flourish of his hand.

"M'lady," he teased, inviting her out.

Karina's eyes lit up in delight. For a moment, Sean thought she might wrap her arms around his neck. "We need to get to the docking bay and steal a ship."

Or maybe not...

"Let me get your cuffs first," he said, grabbing at her wrists. He turned them over and then fiddled for a few moments. She shifted her weight from one foot to the other, waiting.

He frowned. "Hang on. These aren't the same as mine."

Her face fell. "What? Can you still open them?"

"Yeah." He fiddled some more. "I… no."

Right in front of their eyes, the cuffs seemed to morph as if they had some kind of organic-technology component to them. Two metallic-looking, leaf-like pieces of material grew from the underside of her wrists and wrapped themselves around and over the original metal bracelets.

Sean's eyes boggled as he watched this strange tech. "That's some weird tamper-proofing going on."

"What are we going to do?" Karina asked, her voice an octave higher as she stepped back, trying to get away from the bracelets that bound her.

His eyes still fixated on the cuffs, Sean shook his head. "We need to get you out of here. Let's move."

They turned to head down the passageway to the exit when the sound of footsteps started reverberating through the holding area.

"Shit!" He pushed her back against the wall and out of sight of the corridor. "Someone's coming!"

He looked around for something to improvise with, carefully getting out of the line of sight, too. "I need a gun!" he hissed as loudly as he dared.

Karina casually produced one from her pants pocket.

Sean looked at her in disbelief as he grabbed the weapon from her restrained hands. "You're kidding me?"

She shrugged. "I like to keep one close... for comfort."

Sean, confused, took the gun and wiped his face quickly. "Back," he mouthed, pushing her back farther away from the corner of the wall and then pressing himself against it out of sight, too.

The guard's pace quickened as he approached, presumably realizing that something was wrong. Sean bided his time until the guard appeared, gun and outstretched arms first, around the corner. Without missing a beat, Sean grabbed them and turfed the cyborg over and onto his back.

The guard screamed in a slightly falsetto fashion, amusing the pair of escapees.

"Wow," Sean commented, taking his gun off him and shoving it into his waistband. "Did you get your voice enhanced at the same time as your reaction times?"

Provoked and still shocked, the guard struggled and started shouting out. Sean stomped on his throat, silencing him and preoccupying his hands as he gasped for breath. Sean felt a slight crunch under his boot.

"There goes his trachea," he mused grimly.

A second later, another guard appeared at the end of the passageway, this time shooting as he approached. Sean didn't hesitate. He returned fire, distracted for a moment. When he looked back at the guard under his foot, he realized that Karina had shot the guard through the chest. "Was that really necessary?" he scolded her.

Karina shrugged, dangling yet another pistol she'd managed to keep hidden from their captors. "How else are we going to get out of here?" she shot back. "You wanna tie them all up as we go?"

Sean sighed, laser fire still coming down the corridor from at least two more guards. He pressed himself against the wall. "Honestly, women!" he chuffed casually, despite them still being under fire. "Hang on..."

Karina stepped back, watching Sean as he cockily fired his own weapon back down the corridor, allowing his cyborg reflexes and spatial memory to pick their attackers off one by one, with surgical precision.

"Ugh."

"Ugh."

"Ugh." *Slump.*

He looked around the wall to check he'd got them all and then came out of hiding, helping Karina step over the dead body. "Okay, let's move."

"How did you—"

"I'm a very good shot," he said flatly, moving quickly ahead, gun up again, sweeping their path.

Karina followed. They headed out to the elevator. Sean did a quick check around and, deciding it was their best option, hit the call button.

Karina eyed him critically. "You realize there are going to be a bunch of guards in this elevator?"

Sean nodded sharply and stood to the side. He gestured for her to do the same. The elevator doors slid open, and guards armed to the hilt started piling out. Sean effortlessly picked them off one by one.

Karina almost looked impressed, he noticed.

He stepped inside, seeing one guy already collapsed against the back of the tin can.

Karina frowned, hands on hips. "What happened to him?"

"Bonehead must have forgotten this is bulletproof," he said, tapping the wall of the anti-grav elevator cart. "He must have tried to fire at us through the walls! Like I said: bonehead."

The pair stepped inside.

Karina hit the buttons to get them to the lower docking level while Sean pushed the bodies out of the car and then out of the way of the doors.

The doors slid closed, trapping them for the duration of their journey.

Sean watched in mounting anticipation as the lights lit up, one floor number after another, taking them lower and lower in the space station. He checked his pulse discreetly so that Karina wouldn't notice. It was steady.

His shoulders relaxed.

I'm right at home, under fire, escaping with a damsel in distress, he thought to himself.

The elevator stopped, and the pair readied themselves, pointing their weapons at the opening doors.

The doors opened, revealing a surprised family of Skaine: two grown-ups and two kids. Sean frowned, cocked his head, then lowered his weapon. "Sorry," he grunted, stepping past them and into the spartan corridor. Karina followed, smiling and bobbing her head politely.

"Mommy, why are they carrying guns, and why is that girl in handcuffs?" a little voice asked as they passed the family by.

Karina could hear one of the grown-ups explaining to the innocent: "You'll know when you're older."

As soon as they were both clear of the family, they started jogging, heading down the corridor, looking for any signs that would point them toward the docking bay.

"You know how to hot-jack a ride?" Karina called in a loud whisper through the concrete corridors.

Sean turned back to her. "Yeah, I can." His tone was just as cocky as ever.

I'm on a damn roll!

Karina was panting now, as she had to run twice as hard to keep up. "How do you know how to do that?"

Sean hesitated. "I... I don't remember," he faltered. "But I know I can!" he added confidently.

As long as my amazing luck doesn't run out.

"Ok, hot shot," she called. "This way. I think this is the docking bay that family came from. We could do with something without military grade encryption."

Sean had been a couple of paces ahead. He had to stop suddenly and turn back to make the turn she had just taken. He heard a door slam somewhere in the corridors. Seconds later, there were footsteps behind them. "Shit, I think we've been found!" he announced.

"Fuck!" Karina hissed. "Maybe we can lose them in the docking bay."

Just then, a team of armed guards appeared from an adjoining corridor ahead of them.

Karina slowed her pace to a walk. Sean did the same, then

turned to see another pack of cyborgs with guns catching up to them.

"Any ideas?" Karina asked, her attitude suddenly nonexistent.

Sean shook his head. He could feel tension rising in his chest. Suddenly, without any other warning cues, he felt his arms and legs go dead. He was paralyzed to the spot. The teams were closing in on them, in front and behind.

And they looked angry.

As in, murderously angry.

Karina put her hands up as best she could, still being cuffed. "Sean? What do we do? Sean?"

Sean couldn't move. He tried to speak and found it hard to even move his jaw.

This was it. This was how the life of Sean Royale ends...

"Sean."

"Sean?"

"Sean!"

"Are you asleep? I'm talking to you."

Sean felt himself waking up, adrenaline shooting through his system. He tried to move and found himself uncomfortably slouched on a hard floor with his back against something hard. His hands were cuffed again.

He opened his eyes to find himself back in Don Calzone's study. He was sitting on the floor across from Karina, who was still leafing through catalogs.

"I need an answer, Sean. Should we go with the petrilia pink or the skylight blue napkins?"

It all came rushing back to him. *This* was their escape plan. And it was almost too much to bear.

So much for waking up from a nightmare, he thought to himself.

CHAPTER NINE

Calzone Offices, Bronislovas Trading Outpost, Kirox Quadrant

"Ohhhhhhh," Karina cooed as if she were in seventh heaven. "This. Is. Incredible!"

Sean called over to her from the corner. "It's cake, Karina. How good can it be?"

Karina put another piece into her mouth, savoring the sensations. She picked up the card that lay next to it. "Says here, it's specifically designed as an aphrodisiac for most mammalian species."

Without even looking up from his console, Vito gruffed from across the room. "What does it do to the reptilians? I don't want them keeling over at the reception. Bad for business."

Karina kept reading. "Doesn't say. Though, I don't suppose they'd be allowed to sell it if it were toxic to them."

Vito grunted something under his breath and carried on with what he was doing.

"I'll make a note to find out, though," she muttered, glancing over anxiously, trying to appease him. She tapped a note on her holo.

She looked over the table, piled high with cake samples and catalogs, and then at Sean. He was slouched on the floor, back against the sofa, his hands in cuffs, and looking more tormented than if her father had actually ordered up someone to torture him with tools. Or waterboarding.

She smiled. "Looks like they can make this one look like a spaceship. I think that would be quite romantic, don't you?"

Sean sighed. "How is a spaceship wedding cake romantic?"

"You know, because that's how you rescued me."

Sean huffed. "Why don't we just go the whole hog and have some little sugared figurines made up of you and me? You can be all bound, and I can be carrying you off into the spaceship cake." He brightened as he talked. Making digs at her seemed to perk him up.

The Don reeled around from his console. "We'll have none of that!" he ordered sternly. "Need I remind you that this is my daughter you're talking about? Have you already forgotten your place?"

Sean's boredom got the better of his patience. "How could I forget?" he growled back. "These handcuffs are a constant reminder!"

Karina glanced from one to the other, like a spectator at a tennis match. Quickly, she intervened. "Here Sean, try this one," she told him, walking over to him with a plate with some cake samples on it.

"I'd rather try the champagne," he grumbled.

She shook her head, pushing a forkful of cake at him. "That won't be here until later. They're importing samples from the Furuga District."

"Well, I could drink anything. Anything that will help me deal with this!" He gestured at his bound wrists and then to the room in general.

Karina squatted down next to him. "Come on," she cajoled. "It's not that bad."

She leaned in closer, lowering her voice. "You don't want to anger him. He might easily decide to put us both back into his dungeon."

"At least get him to take these cuffs off," he pleaded. "They're uncomfortable."

Karina nodded. "Daddy?"

She waited for her father to look up. "What, princess? Daddy's working."

"Daddy," she repeated coyly. "Please, may we take Sean's handcuffs off? I promise he'll be good."

Vito thought for a moment and then his expression hardened. "You know we can't do that until you're married," he ruled.

Sean couldn't keep his mouth shut any longer. "You're going to have me stand at the altar in cuffs? Won't your guests be a bit suspicious?"

Vito rocked back in his console chair. "No, not at all," he said casually. "They're used to it."

Karina looked resigned. "He's right," she agreed. "Once, he had a guy killed at his own funeral. It was messy. Blood all over the casket."

Sean's mind whirred, trying to process what she'd just said. "You mean…"

"Yeah. Announced the funeral and had him lie down in the box after he'd said goodbye to his family and friends."

Sean's mouth dropped open. "That's… awful!"

Vito sat up. "Actually, I was being kind. I gave him a chance to say goodbye to everyone. When does anyone ever get that opportunity?"

Sean tried to cover his face with his retrained hands. "But he knew he was going to die. And so did everyone else!"

Vito protested casually. "It was the humane thing to do. He'd served me well for twenty years."

Sean couldn't believe what he was hearing. "Shit," he muttered, making eye contact with Karina, who seemed to have nothing to offer the conversation. "I'd hate to see what you do to your enemies."

Karina suddenly burst out laughing, shooting crumbs all over the carpet in front of them. "He used to joke about having them married off to his wayward daughter!"

Sean glared. "Well, I can see now that that makes sense."

"Oh, come on," she said, nudging him playfully. "Don't be such a party pooper. This is going to be fun. After we've chosen the cake, we still have so many decisions to make, like flowers and table ornaments and…"

Sean had already stopped listening and was imagining he was back in his nightmare, trying to figure out how to break out of the corridor.

Because anything, including certain death from a team of assassins, was better than this…

Paige's office, Safehouse, Gaitune-67

The safehouse beyond her office was deadly silent, offering no assistance to the dilemma the pair faced.

Paige sat quietly, poised at her desk, waiting for Gareth Jones to respond. Even through the holo medium, she could see that he was perplexed. The normally friendly, smiling eyes looked stressed and strained now as he considered the information she had just shared with him.

"I must admit," he said finally, "I'm somewhat baffled by this."

"Me too," Paige agreed. "I've called around a few other admin departments at similar institutions. No one has heard of an investigation like this before."

"I just don't get it. Maybe it's a clerical error? They have no reason to investigate." He stroked his chin. "And they didn't tell you anything else?"

Paige shook her head.

Gareth sighed and leaned back in his anti-grav chair. "There's no reason for it. I was extra careful with the paperwork in having the university registered as a place of education. All the filings have been done on time and by the book. I suppose…" he paused, as if hardly daring to speak the words, "the issue may be political in nature."

Paige frowned but waited for him to explain.

Gareth shrugged and leaned forward again, this time with a twist in his lips as if he were in pain. "It's no secret that the content of our courses is controversial. Promoting peace and cooperation on a planet-wide scale alone is going to hit a lot of industries hard."

Paige pursed her lips. "I was afraid that was the conclusion we might be left with. Have we any way to find out for sure?"

Gareth shook his head. "Not really. I can put a few calls in and see if any of my contacts have heard anything. It'll all be hearsay though, and there's no way to use anything I learn to stop it."

Paige wrinkled her nose. "Bummer. So, anything we can do about stopping it any other way? Through the courts perhaps?"

Gareth scratched his face, thinking. "I suppose… You see, the thing is, because this hasn't happened before, there is nothing to compare it to. And so, there is no precedent. By extension, there is no precedent to getting it overturned, either. Bottom line, since it is a private facility with customers and so on, the government will always be able to argue it has a right to protect its citizens."

"So, we can't stop them?" Paige's spine slumped as she felt the exhaustion of the whole matter catch up to her. She'd spent all morning on calls trying to find some loophole or way out of the investigation.

"We can try," Gareth said quietly. Paige noticed the lack of optimism in his voice, though. "I'll get someone onto it, but I think realistically, they're going to do what they want to do."

Paige had to know. "And what do you think their endgame is?"

"Worst case? Shut us down."

"And best case is that they get something they can use to manipulate us?" Paige asked.

Gareth nodded grimly. His complexion was looking pasty now. "Sounds like you know how the bigger picture gets played."

Paige tried to smile. "I've had some experience."

Gareth nodded gently. "Okay. Let's stay in touch. I'll let you know as soon as I find anything at this end, but as it stands, it looks like they're going to end up doing that investigation. All we can hope then is that they don't end up finding anything."

Paige held her hand up to wave. "Okay, then. Thanks, Gareth. We'll be in touch."

The call ended, and Paige sat staring into space for several moments, replaying the conversation in her mind. She closed the open holoscreens, her eye catching again on the holocomm from Info Corp. Her stomach sank.

This is too much to deal with, she thought to herself as she grabbed her empty mocha mug and headed out of the door, with the full weight of the university and her company on her shoulders.

Aboard *The ArchAngel*, Sark System

Carol stomped her way along the corridors of *The ArchAngel*, her arm held by her husband and escorted by a pair of armed guards.

"Oh, for goodness sake, this is ridiculous!" she spat, struggling to release herself from Philip's grip. He held firm.

"Come on, where am I going to run to?" she insisted.

Philip eyed her carefully. He maintained a cool exterior. The exterior she had thought of as sexy when he was out on missions. Right now, though, she could see the cracks appearing. She could tell he was having second thoughts. She also suspected he was somewhat embarrassed to be doing this. Whether that was in the face of the Federation, or her, she couldn't quite figure out.

"Just stop struggling," he told her firmly. "We've all made the mistake of underestimating you before." He broke into a tiny smile before adding, "You should take that as a compliment."

Carol stopped struggling. "Look, let me just walk, and I'll make this easy. We don't have to be… uncivilized."

Philip sighed and released her. She continued to walk but straightened herself up and corrected her posture, now walking with dignity. Philip shook his head to himself. *She was determined and proud, if nothing else…*

Carol continued talking, by way of a thank you. "You realize I despise this man," she muttered quietly so that the escorts couldn't hear. Or so she assumed.

Philip glanced at her briefly, acknowledging the statement but saying nothing.

Eventually, they arrived on the corridor they needed to be on, and the guards took them into the office. The door swooshed open, allowing them to step through into a rather comfortable looking office suite. Lance appeared, ambling casually from his side office.

"Philip, Carol, good of you to come," he greeted them, stepping forward. Philip and Lance shook hands and exchanged pleasantries.

Carol glared at Lance before holding her bound wrists up. "I'd shake your hand, but it seems my husband would rather I stayed restrained for the duration of my kidnapping."

Lance wandered over to her. "Hello, Carol. I'm sorry about the methods. I just needed to be sure to get you up here. And I know we have a difficult relationship, so I didn't think you'd come easily."

He glanced at Philip, who remained silent, watching as Lance took the blame for his methods.

Carol straightened her posture indignantly. Philip imagined the hackles on the back of her neck going up as she spoke. "By difficult relationship, you mean that you admit that you're an overbearing nincompoop who thinks he can throw his Federation authority all over the place and expects everyone else to just fall in line?"

Lance smiled coolly as he wandered over to his drinks tray. He poured a drink for each of them and handed them out. Carol, surprisingly, took hers gracefully, despite having her hands bound.

"I hear you've been monitoring Molly," he said, more as an opening statement than a question.

"That's right," she said. "I have a duty to my planet to monitor all threats. And as a parent, I need to make sure my daughter isn't caught up in any Federation… shenanigans… that are going to get her killed."

"Well, that's unfortunate because it looks like you're having the exact opposite effect." Lance regarded her sternly. "Your daughter has gone off to the Kirox Quandrant, where we have absolutely no influence, I might add, in an attempt to find Sean Royale, who is now missing and probably dead. Want to explain what you know of this?"

Carol's eyes narrowed, and her face darkened. "That Sean Royale is the reason we're having this conversation. I know his type. He's bad news. And he's all wrapped up with Molly. I'm just protecting my daughter."

Lance glanced over at Philip. "What exactly did she do?"

Philip shuffled his feet and took a swig of the Yollin Brandy Lance had just handed him. "Reading between the lines, I think Carol sent an ex-operative off to ensnare him. Get him married so that he's out of the picture and keep him that way."

"I see," Lance mulled.

Carol protested, "I found chatter that points to specific threats against Molly during my investigations, I'll have you know. People coming at her through the university."

Philip's eyebrows jumped in surprise. He said nothing.

Carol continued. "If I hadn't been keeping an eye on things, we would never know, and then where would she be? Having to fake her own death… again. Or worse!"

Philip stood quietly, watching the interaction play out, wondering if Carol was just spouting paranoid conclusions… or whether something was actually afoot. He regarded Lance carefully, looking for signs of him knowing about these threats. The man wasn't giving anything away. He remained his normally calm and collected self.

Lance didn't ask any questions, either. Instead, he waved a finger to one of the guards. "Carol, how about you go with Bill and relax for a little while so I can talk with your husband?"

Carol looked at the two guards waiting to escort her. "What, you're *dismissing* me?" she asked in a raised voice. "You have my husband break all kinds of laws and vows and bring me up here to—"

One of the guards went to take her by the arm. She pulled away violently, then composed herself. "I can walk," she said angrily. And then without another word, she strode out of the room, followed by her two escorts.

"Where are they taking her?" Philip asked nervously.

Lance waved a hand. "Just somewhere to cool off. Let's you and I go and grab some dinner. I've not eaten all day." He closed down some holos on his desk and then headed across the office suite to Philip, before inviting him to step out of the door ahead of him.

Philip walked ahead, his mind churning. He glanced back at Lance as they stepped out into the corridor. "Sir, what if there really are other threats against Molly? In her position, Carol could help. And I've no doubt she's looking out for her."

Lance nodded, then put a finger to his lips. "This is classified, but we *will* talk," he promised as he led the way down the corridor. "Let's go eat."

Philip shifted his food around his plate, barely registering that he should be eating. "I feel bad knowing you've got her locked up somewhere," he confessed to Lance, who seemed perfectly composed and content.

"Locked up?" Lance repeated. "Oh, no. I'm sure she's fine. ADAM, give us a visual on Mrs. Bates please."

A holoscreen pulled itself up in the middle of the dining table. It showed a spa setting, complete with a small pool and hot tubs around.

"Punch in," Lance commanded.

The viewer zoomed in on two women sitting with face masks on sun loungers. Philip recognized the type of drink they had from the shape of the glasses. "That's Carol?" he asked.

Lance nodded, putting another forkful of food in his mouth.

"And the other lady?"

"Barb Kurns," Lance relayed. "The two of them met at some counterintelligence conference or other. Thought Carol might be more forthcoming to someone who wasn't me."

Philip raised his eyebrows and then nodded. "And after a couple of martinis…" he observed.

"Quite," Lance agreed, a mischievous glimmer in his eye.

"So, you really did send her to cool off…"

"Yeah. Those women, they'll blow off steam gossiping and sharing and then be able to have a reasonable conversation."

"So, you think that Carol actually has something?"

Lance nodded, glancing around to make sure there was no one else within earshot. "I do," he confided. "I'd like to see the intel she's uncovered, but we have our own suspicions about something in play."

"Like what?"

"Well, we've noticed big shifts in the market. Moves of

money... without any news or triggers that would influence market dynamics."

Philip frowned, placing his fork down. "You suspect insider trading?"

"Oh, no... well, there may be some of that. But it more suggests to us that there is something else going on behind the scenes that we're not fully privy to."

"Okay. You say that like there's more?"

"There is," Lance confirmed. "We've noticed a certain rearrangement in the military. Like promotions happening that are... idiosyncratic. Appointments that are unexpected from our models. It suggests a changing political landscape and a shift in power."

"In favor of?"

"Well, that's what we're in the process of figuring out. We haven't been able to pinpoint it, which is why it's important for us to look at whatever data Carol has collected."

Philip's eyes were alight with interest. "So, you think there is a movement happening?"

"I do. And we need to be ready for it. You and Carol have served your planet well. You've been loyal to the common good. I feel we can trust you. And as ambassadors for your planet, I hope we can work together more closely to deal with this potential threat."

Philip's eyes glazed over as he looked at his plate. "You realize I'm retired."

Lance smiled. "Yes. I know that feeling well too, myself. But there is more to do. And your daughter is undoubtedly going to be at the center of whatever needs doing... so..." He kept eating for a few minutes, giving Philip time to think.

"Anyway," Lance said eventually, "I figured that you and I were better off out of the picture for now. Given that she detests me, and given you kidnapped her to bring her up here, I thought it best."

Philip nodded and started eating. "Yes, very clever," he agreed.

"We'll just let Barb do her thing," he said, closing the holo-screen and checking the time on his holo. "She'll mellow her out. We just need to wait."

CHAPTER TEN

<u>Aboard *The Empress*, Glom Space station, Kirox Quadrant</u>

Molly stood in the center of the lounge, guns strapped to her legs, in mission-mode. "Okay, folks, listen up. What we know is that Scamp last docked here for four days, arriving with Sean, leaving without him. We know that Sean was here. He might still be, so we're looking for anything that can give us a clue as to his whereabouts now."

She nodded at Pieter. "Pieter, you and I are going to hack the station's security feeds and scan for any footage of him."

She looked to the others one by one as she issued the orders. "The rest of you, head out there and blend in. No gunfights. No fisticuffs. Just blend. And see what you can find out. Do people get twitchy if you ask about a human cyborg out here? Has anyone seen him? Have a story… like he is your friend or brother. Try and keep any mention of the Federation, or our military operation and capabilities, out of it. This is enemy territory potentially. We have no idea what we're walking in to, and this is a damn long way to get help from the Federation out here."

She noticed the solemn looks on their faces. "And one more thing," she added. "If anyone is capable of finding Sean alive and well, it's you. You're the best friends a soldier could have. And the most capable team that he's ever known. He told me that once." Her eyes drifted off as if remembering, and then she smirked. "Albeit, he was drinking at the time…"

Everyone chuckled.

"But he meant it," she continued. "He has faith in you. And so do I. Now, let's go get our guy and bring him home." She clapped her hands in a "round em up and move out" way, and everyone hopped to, slinging their gear on their backs and moving to the exit.

"Crash, you stay here and run point."

Crash responded from the doorway and not over the intercom as Molly had expected. "Yes, sir!" he called.

She turned, smiled at him, and then followed the rest of the team off the boat.

There was a muddle of activity as everyone got their bearings. The docking bay was quiet, but there seemed to be many doors and nothing was signposted. It took a few moments for them to find their way to the main corridor that would let them out and onto the station, and then deliberately, they broke up into small teams.

Joel stuck with Molly. "I've got your six," he told her definitively.

Molly was about to argue and then had a better idea. "How about you follow Pieter and me at a distance, in case we run into trouble? Then you're not already accounted for in an attack."

Joel bobbed his head. "Yeah. Good thinking."

She smiled, wanting to tell him how grateful she was for his extra care and attention. But she didn't know what to say. Particularly since Pieter was still in earshot. "Okay," she managed. "Let's move out, Pieter!"

Pieter scrambled to fold away a holoscreen he had been checking and fidgeted with the pack on his back. No doubt he was carrying all kinds of tech they wouldn't need. But Molly was glad that he came prepared.

She strode out along the corridor, following the thoroughfare that the others had already disappeared down. Pieter hurried after her. Joel waited a short time and then followed at a safe distance.

"I managed to take a peek at the general layout," Pieter told Molly, his voice as low as he could make it but still have her hear him. "If I had to guess, I'd say their central hub was going to be on one of the top floors, but near the center of the base."

Molly nodded. "Let's see what Oz can find."

Oz responded almost immediately in their implants. "Pieter was pretty accurate. They're one corridor over from the central concourse. Floor Twenty."

Molly kept walking, following the flow of people into the main living spaces of the ship. Her eyes darted discreetly, looking for signposts and clues to help them get to their destination.

"Don't suppose you can just tap them from where we are? Over their XtraNet?"

"I could. But it will take more time to get to the video footage. I'd be much quicker if you can get one of Pieter's hacking dongles into a port in one of the servers."

Molly sighed. "Nothing can ever be easy."

Pieter smiled. "It will be once we get this bit out of the way. Promise."

Molly shook her head. "Don't jinx it, dude."

Pieter chuckled. "You never struck me as the superstitious kind!"

"I wasn't... until I started falling through realms and realized that nothing is within my control."

Pieter stopped laughing and went quiet, processing the implications of what she'd been through. "I, erm... I'd never thought of it like that."

Molly shrugged. "It's okay. Come on, I think that's an elevator over there." She pointed to an area where people were milling. There were all kinds of species around. She noticed a couple of Zyhn and a whole bunch she didn't recognize. There were even a few humans, which surprised her, them being this far out from what she assumed was human civilization.

They approached the knot of activity and confirmed there was a bay of anti-grav elevators taking people between floors. They waited their turn and eventually got into one that would take them to Floor Twenty. Squishing in next to some rather indelicate creatures that smelled like sewage, they held their breath and tried to avoid eye contact in case anyone noticed their reaction.

Finally, it was their floor. The bad-smelling guys had gotten off the stop before them, but Pieter and Molly still tried not to communicate until they were off the elevator and away into the concourse.

"Ahh, man, there are some weird-ass creatures out here!" Pieter hissed.

Molly smirked discreetly. Though she agreed about the uncomfortable smell, it wasn't time for a debate on tolerance and acceptance. "This way," she muttered, moving off in the direction Oz had told her.

Pieter scurried after her, realizing how long her legs were. *I've never noticed that before,* he mused to himself, completely distracted from the mission briefly.

There weren't quite as many people on this floor, and it seemed like it might hold offices rather than the high streets and trading markets these space stations were normally known for. Molly guessed it was probably a station administration floor.

She made a beeline for a set of double doors which took them onto an even quieter corridor. She walked quickly but as stealthily as she could. Arriving at their destination, she leaned gently against the third door along, pressing down on the handle. It was locked.

Oz. Bit of help here? Can you override the door lock?

One sec.

She glanced furtively down the corridor. Pieter knelt down and pretended to be fixing his boot strap.

Something clicked in the door, and Molly pushed again. The door opened, and she slipped inside, followed by Pieter.

Pieter watched, everything happening in slow motion. He hadn't considered that there would be guards in a server room. But then, as he took in the scene, it was obvious that it was also the control room. One of the guards was Skaine. He only guessed this from some pictures in a Federation presentation he'd flicked through during his induction. He was tall and mean-looking, with full body armor and blue skin.

The other two were human, but enhanced with robotic attachments and overpumped muscles. Cyborgs. Pieter's mind told him to reach for his weapon. But his arms were slow to obey. He felt his muscles freeze up.

As he fought his own paralysis, he also watched Molly react effortlessly and rapidly. Not only had she already slipped her guns from her holsters, but she'd bumped them on each of her arms. He guessed she was knocking the safeties off.

Then she fired.

Pop. Pop. *Bang.*

Graceful. Quiet.

The three guards went down.

All in the same stride, she moved forward and busied herself with the panels. She was talking to him, but he couldn't hear her. His hearing was muffled, and everything was still happening in slow motion. Except his thinking.

She needed something from him.

She was looking directly at him now. Asking him a question. Suddenly, time snapped back to normal.

"Are you okay, Pieter?"

"Yeah... sorry. Yeah, I'm fine... I..."

"I need the dongle for Oz," Molly said. Pieter got the sense this wasn't the first time she had asked.

"Oh, right." He rummaged in his backpack, remembering he'd put it somewhere safe and accessible. A second later, he realized it was in his pants pocket. He pulled it out and handed it over to her, fumbling every move.

Molly took the drive and plugged it into the computer, hitting holoscreens and moving the code to help Oz.

A moment later, she pulled the drive out again and got up. "Time to go."

Pieter was still dazed. "Don't we want to look at the footage?"

Molly was already halfway to the door. "Not here. Oz is into the system now and can work over the XtraNet."

Pieter mouthed "Oh" and then realized he needed to get the hell out of there, too. He turned on his heels and followed Molly's atmosuit down to the elevators again.

"What's going on with you?" she whispered under her breath as they awaited the anti-grav cart's arrival.

"Sorry. I erm… I think the technical term is I lost my shit."

Molly smiled at him and threw her arm around his shoulders. "You did great, fella. Field work is always a bit intense."

There was no one about. Pieter blurted out what was on his mind. "Those guards. You took them out without even pausing. Before I even knew what was happening!" Despite his whisper, his voice was about two octaves higher than normal.

Molly shrugged. "Training. Plus, I've been under fire a lot more than you have."

Pieter watched the cart arrive at their level. "Did you… kill them?"

Molly shook her head and showed him the settings on the gun. He bobbed his head, understanding now what she'd done when she whacked them on her arms before firing. It wasn't the safety she was knocking off. She was adjusting the settings down to stun.

"Hang on then," he whispered, suddenly putting it all together. "How long have we got before they wake up?"

Molly stuck her bottom lip out. "Dunno... maybe... ten minutes?"

Pieter's mouth dropped open.

Molly chuckled and closed it again for him with a gentle finger under his chin.

The elevator arrived, and the doors opened to reveal Joel standing there, looking amused with a holo up as if he were reading something. "Everything okay?" he asked casually.

Molly nodded. "All fine. We need to get out of here soon, though." She and Pieter stepped into the cart.

Joel noticed Pieter's normally pale complexion was positively gray. He put a hand on his shoulder in support, and the elevator doors closed behind them to whisk them back down to the market concourse.

"Guess we better hope the others found something then," Joel said wryly. He narrowed his eyes at Molly. "Did you just kill someone?"

"No, that's the hurry," she explained. "They're going to wake up."

Joel shrugged. "If you had, then all hell would break loose trying to find a killer on base. Good call."

Molly tilted her head and then watched out of the window as the elevator descended.

Base conference room, Gaitune-67

Maya flicked excitedly between one holoscreen to another, comparing results. The audio in the conference room was playing an archived news report about the Newstainment takeover. She lifted her gaze from the screens only when she heard Paige's high heels announcing her arrival at the door.

Maya grinned. "How you doing?" she asked brightly.

Paige shook her head. "Not as well as you, it seems." She was carrying two mocha cups. She headed over to Maya's side of the table and placed one down in front of her. "Extra frothy, extra hot." She smiled.

"Thanks, hon!" Maya pulled the lid off and poked her nose into the cup, savoring the aroma. Remembering the recording playing in the background, she poked at a screen and paused it.

"What you listening to?" Paige asked.

"Newstainment takeover," Maya explained, realizing the mocha was too hot to drink straight away. "Turns out, it was a hostile takeover. Info Corp bought up just shy of fifteen percent of the shares in the open market before they made the approach. Timing was bad too. The Newstainment group released a bad earnings report, and then a series of really bad news reports dropped their share price. Made it easy for Info Corp to swoop in and pick up the company for a song."

Paige pulled out one of the anti-grav chairs. Her skin was gray again, despite taking the previous night off. "Well, mine isn't a publicly owned company, so they can't try any of that shit with me."

Maya could tell that Paige was thinking about the other ways someone with money and power might be able to get to her. It wasn't going to be productive to contemplate that right now, though. She stayed on track. "So, I did some more digging on Info Corp."

Paige seemed to gather her focus and looked directly at Maya, giving her her full attention. "What did you find?"

"Well, it looks like Info Corp is indeed a shelf company, as I suspected."

"You mean a shell company?"

Maya shook her head decisively. "Nope. A *shelf* company, my non-criminally-minded friend. It's a company that has history but no traceable activity. Cultivated and filed for years and years until it's sold to someone dodgy for dodgy activities. Criminals use them to make a company look legit to anyone who isn't looking too carefully. But there are telltale signs. Add into the mix that apart from funding the accounts and a few spurious transactions, Info Corp only started buying up shares in other companies months ago."

Paige frowned. "How could you possibly know that? They won't have filed any accounts yet, if that's the case… and how did you see their transactions?"

Maya waved her hand. "Ways. You don't need to know the details. But," she added, the investigative journalist glint back in her eyes, "the most interesting bit is where I traced the source of the funds to."

Paige leaned forward, clearly moved by Maya's enthusiasm. "Tell me," she pressed.

Maya grinned. "It's a privately held fund called the Northern Clan of Cambodian."

"Sounds Ogg."

"It is," Maya confirmed. "Money from a few of the wealthiest clans out there."

Paige frowned. "So, we've got Ogg money wanting to influence affairs in Estaria?"

Maya nodded. "Seems so."

"What do we know about them?"

"Not much. Their site is sparse. Vague even."

"You think you might be able to get some real intel on these guys?"

Maya tilted her head and looked back at her screen as if assessing the problem. "I can give it a good try."

"Okay great." Paige pulled up her own holoscreens. "I'll see what I can find out about the other acquisitions in the group."

The pair were quiet as they worked away for a few minutes. Paige took a sip of her mocha and then seemed to have a thought. "Hey, Maya?"

"Yeah?" Maya didn't look up right away. Then she did.

Paige's face looked taut with stress again. "You know, your guy at Newstainment might have some theories. Think we can reach out to him?"

Maya bit her bottom lip. "It's risky. I mean, I'm not meant to be around anymore." She thought for a moment more. "But if anyone is going to have an inside beat on it, he would. Lemme think about how to loop him in. It might be a case of having to show up on his doorstep to avoid raising any flags in the comms."

Paige nodded. "Yeah. Of course. And I can do the door-stepping if that's safer, too."

Maya bobbed her head, and the pair fell silent again, poking at their holoscreens, trying to figure out what they'd stumbled upon.

Glom Space station, Kirox Quadrant

Jack sat in the bar across the street from the barber's shop. Legs crossed in a ladylike way and her hair down, she could almost pass as a civilian.

Almost.

The waitress put her beer on the table, along with the bill.

"What happened over there?" Jack asked, nodding at a broken table shoved in one corner.

The waitress rolled her eyes. "Some kind of kidnapping."

Jack frowned. "Someone was kidnapped?"

"Yeah. Some girl. Cyborgs. Wasn't my shift, though." She walked away, completely disinterested in sharing the story.

Jack hit her comm and reported it to Joel.

"Okay, be ready to leave in a few," he responded into her audio implant. "Molly and Pieter are on their way back down with me now. Where's Brock?"

"Well, he's in the middle of an edge up," she said, peering out the window across the street and into the barber's shop.

"A what?"

"An edge up."

"Come again?"

"He's in the barber shop. He's almost done."

"Can you get word to him that we need to leave?"

"Not without being suspicious. I can tell him through his comm, but if he's talking to someone, he won't be able to answer. And we kinda don't want to spook whomever he's pumping for intel."

"Okay. Do what you can. Meet us back at the newsstand before the dock corridor."

"Roger that," Jack said quietly, clicking the bill against her holo scanner to pay it.

She sat for another few moments, drinking her beer, before she surreptitiously hit her implant to speak with Brock.

Brock heard the call coming in. He pretended to scratch an itch behind his ear.

"Molly and Pieter have what they need. We need to move soon."

Brock double clicked the implant, still pretending to scratch and then disconnected the call. He knew out of anyone on the team, Jack was most likely to understand the acknowledgment.

"So, what do you think happened to him?" Brock asked, continuing his conversation with the barber as he tidied up the last bit of hair from his neck.

"I don't know for sure. Word on the street is that he's not going to get away from the Don that easily. Not again."

"Where is he now, then?"

The barber sucked air through his teeth, grimacing. "Well, if he's not in shackles, he'll be dead. That's for sure. Once the boss sets his mind to something, that's it. Game over."

Brock tried not to let his concern show. "So, you think he's got him holed up somewhere then?"

"Well, we know the big event is going to be happening at the weekend. And it will happen at the big church over on the trading post."

Brock carefully took mental notes, putting together the clues. "Yeah?"

"Yeah," the barber continued talking. "I hear it's all going down at high noon. It's going to be quite the occasion. All the local criminal families are being invited to see it."

"To see what?"

"You know…" The barber drew his finger across his throat. "Like I said. Game over."

Brock's eyes widened. "Where do you think he's being held until then?"

"Not sure. Probably on the same outpost, though. I mean, there are all the preparations to do, and frankly, when you've got something like that coming up, there isn't much else you should be doing elsewhere, right?" He chuckled, slapping Brock on the shoulder as if he'd just cracked the funniest joke in the world. Then, he reached up to his collar, peeled off the gown, and allowed his customer out of his seat.

Brock, stunned, got up. He dusted himself down and headed over to the cashier. "Right. Of course. Thank you."

He paid for the haircut and, half dazed, ambled out into the street. He saw Jack coming out of the restaurant across the way and met her on the street.

"This way," she muttered discreetly, leading the way back to the rendezvous point.

Brock followed, eager to share his news as soon as it was safe.

Brock moved quickly down the corridor, trying to keep pace with Jack who seemed overly agitated.

"Hey," he called quietly. "Slow down! What's going on?"

Jack slowed just long enough for him to hear her speak. "Two station guards were talking into their earpieces and then looked our way out on the street. They're following us."

Brock felt a shot of adrenaline plow through his system. "Shit."

"Exactly. We need to move."

With that, she increased her pace, making it more difficult for Brock to keep up. "By my ancestors, if I get out of this alive, I'll spend more time in the gym. I promise!"

He pushed his legs as fast as they could move without breaking out into a run. Jack disappeared around a corner ahead of him. He rounded it a few seconds later to see Molly, Pieter, and Joel waiting anxiously by the newsstand in the corner of a crossroads to several corridors leading to various docks. Molly saw him arrive and started moving the others to the next corridor.

Brock approached. "They're right behind me," he hissed. Molly nodded and pushed him along to follow the others. When he turned back, he saw the guards had arrived around the corner, weapons drawn.

Molly drew her pistol, too, and without a second thought, fired at the pair. One was hit and went down. The other ducked back behind the corner.

"*Run!*" she ordered. Brock heard the others ahead of him break into a run. He followed, scared out of his wits.

"Shiiiiiiiitttt!" he squealed involuntarily.

Before he knew it, Molly was racing alongside him. "Come on. We've got to move. More are on their way."

As if to prove her point, a laser blast whistled past his ear, causing him to jump midstride and almost fall over. He kept running, his feet pounding deliberately on the ground to help him regain his balance.

Molly had stopped and popped off several more shots. At the next corner, Brock glanced back to see her taking cover behind a recess in the wall, still shooting and taking down one guard at a time. He didn't notice how many guards were coming after them now, but there was a lot of laser fire bouncing around the corridors.

Panic flooded his whole body. He noticed the others disappear into a dock. He hoped it was the right one and then dove in after them.

"Where's Molly?" Joel demanded.

Brock looked back at the door. "She was right behind me."

Joel waved the others onto the ship. "Emma?" he said hitting his comm, "get powered up and ready to leave. We're under fire." He turned to Brock. "Get on board. I'll get Molly."

And with that, Joel pulled out his weapon from his leg holster and strode back out of the door and immediately started laying down fire.

Brock shook his head in amazement and then followed the others up the invisible steps to get on board so they wouldn't impede Joel and Molly's path.

Brock arrived in the cockpit and immediately started helping Crash prep for takeoff.

"Emma, can you override the docking clamps?" he asked within a second of his butt hitting the seat.

"Who are you talking to?" she teased confidently.

"Okay, and how about helping those two get on board under fire?" he added.

Emma's visual representation appeared on the screen next to him. "Of course." She winked.

Molly and Joel emerged, walking backwards and shooting as they came into the dock. Joel slammed the dock door behind them and did his best to lock it. Then the pair raced up the stairs.

"Emma, you're up!" Molly shouted as she fell through the door of the ship, closely followed by a rather sweaty Joel, who had to step over her to get to safety.

The door closed automatically behind them, just as the door to the dock opened and in spilled half a dozen guards: Skaine, Zyhn, and cyborg, all firing their weapons at the ship.

Emma had already activated the shields and was decoupling from the dock.

Brock glanced at his screen. "Uh oh," he muttered.

Crash gritted his teeth. "It's okay. We can fly through it if we need to."

Molly scrambled to her feet and followed Joel into the cockpit.

"What's 'uh oh'?" Joel asked.

Molly was the one to respond. "It's okay. Oz is on it. He just needs a minute."

"We haven't got a minute!" Brock squealed.

"*Why?*" Joel asked, raising his voice to be heard over the activity and panic. "What's happening?"

"It's the door behind us," Molly explained. "They've closed it to stop us escaping. Oz is working on the override."

The guard's laser blasts hit against the ship's shields, lighting it up in spots of green light which ran over the surface like spider legs before dispersing.

Anytime now, Oz.

Working on it...

A moment later, *The Empress* pulled away from the dock, and everyone braced for impact with the sealed doors behind them.

"Doors are opening!" Brock announced, checking the visuals on his screen. Crash remained silent, focused on the task at hand.

Joel and Molly relaxed a little, watching with bated breath as the ship reversed out, the spider strikes of the forcefield still occurring regularly and depleting their reserves.

Within a minute, they were out and punching a gate out of range of the station.

"Fuck me, that was close!" Brock chuffed, visibly relieved and breathing hard.

Molly laughed in relief and collapsed dramatically into one of the console chairs between Brock and Crash. "You're telling me!"

Joel noticed a tear in her jacket. "You're hurt."

She glanced down. "Just a graze," she muttered disinterestedly. She sighed and slumped back. "And another perfectly good atmosjacket ruined," she added, realizing the implications.

Brock glanced at her sideways. "That was done saving my ass. When we get back, I'll take you shopping as a thank you."

Molly winked at him. "You're welcome," she said sweetly.

Brock grinned back at her. "Yeah. But we're still going shopping."

"Hmm, something tells me you just want an excuse to shop."

He raised his eyebrows and wiggled them.

They laughed, letting go of the tension of the operation.

"But seriously, I think I discovered something about where to find Sean," Brock said more seriously, swiveling around to face the center of the room and include Joel in the conversation.

Joel perched on the anti-grav chair across from Brock. "What did you find?"

"Well, it seems that Sean is being held somewhere in the next trading post. Something about tomorrow morning, he'll be executed, though. In a church of all places."

Joel frowned. "Sounds… odd. What else do we know?"

Brock shrugged. "Something about the other crime families being present to witness it. I'm guessing Sean has history in this sector… for the Don to want him."

"The Don?" Molly pressed.

"Yeah?"

"As in, a mafia crime family?"

Brock pressed his lips together. "I guess. I couldn't exactly interrogate the guy, though, so I'm kinda filling in the blanks."

The three of them sat in silence, contemplating the new intel.

Crash chirped up, without turning around. "Got coordinates for the nearest trading post. Shall I get us there?"

"Yes," Molly confirmed. "Thanks, Crash. But keep us out of weapons range while we check it out, though."

"Roger that," he reported, punching the holocontrols to get them on their new course.

"The rest of us need to regroup and then saddle up," she announced. "Sounds like we're going into battle. We're going to need to arm up."

Joel was first on his feet again, rubbing his hands together fast. "Let's do this," he muttered with a tone of determination, leading the way out of the cockpit.

Molly followed, all humor and relief now forgotten. It was game time.

Hangar Deck, Gaitune-67

The pod lifted up effortlessly, just like any other time they'd left the base. This time, it was different though: their mood, their mission, and the eerie feeling of being on a ghost base.

Paige glanced over at Maya. "It's going to be okay. We've got this."

"I know." Maya smiled weakly. She looked out of the window as their pod made its way over to the opening hangar doors. "It's just all so different without the others around. And what if something happens? We've no backup."

Paige checked her wrist holo then tapped the hardware. "We've got ArchAngel… in case of a real emergency. Even if we were to just dump a message on a monitored server, she'd respond as quickly as we need her to."

Maya rolled her lips, watching the base disappear beneath

them as they headed for the doors. "Yeah. Not sure I wanna test that theory, though. It's all a bit... hands off... for my tastes."

Paige nudged her playfully. "Check this out. Maya Johnson suddenly concerned about taking risks."

Maya shrugged. "Guess playing with a team has made me soft," she agreed.

Paige rubbed her friend's arm, smiling in amusement. "We'll be back on base before we know it," she promised. "So, what did we find in terms of the best place to intercept Mr. August?"

"Well," Maya started slowly, "it wasn't what I was expecting."

"Oh?"

"Yeah. I looked at his holo movements, and it doesn't look like he's going into the offices anymore."

Paige frowned, not quite comprehending. "What do you mean? He's working from home?"

Maya pressed her lips together firmly. "Not in that role," she replied grimly. "He's mostly been following a routine around his home, apart from going across town once a week and staying out half the night."

"You think he's been fired?"

The pod was now turning and heading off in the direction of Estaria, the onboard EI flicking up basic nav details on the screen and displaying the spacescape behind it on the translucent surface.

"Looks like it," Maya guessed. "I tried scanning company reports and announcements, but there was no mention of them changing their Editor in Chief."

"Would they?"

Maya tilted her head from side to side. "Normally? Maybe. But in the wake of a takeover? Probably not. Not if they wanted to stabilize the stock price or keep the news for an announcement at another time when it might suit them."

Paige shook her head, grabbing onto the hand rail and turning herself to face Maya in the tiny pod. "Never ceases to amaze me… There's just no way to get a bead on what's really going on amongst all this intel."

Maya sighed. "I agree. It's something that Oz was useful for. He's so great when it comes to figuring out probabilities of what's going on."

Paige almost imperceptibly shook her head, as if shaking the regret and wishing from her mind. "Okay, so where does that leave us in terms of our approach?" she asked, refocusing.

Maya pulled up a holo of the area around Bob August's residence to show Paige. "I figured we'd just show up at his apartment and maybe wait for him to emerge… if you didn't want to ring the bell?"

Paige shrugged. "I have no problem ringing the bell. He has no reason to turn us away."

"Unless he's keeping a low profile and doesn't want to be seen with us." She narrowed her eyes conspiratorially.

Paige wanted to tease her about her journalistic streak looking for sensationalism, but deep down, she knew it was a distinct possibility. "Right. Well, if that's the case, we can make it more complicated and get a note to him or something. But let's try the straightforward approach first." She took a look at the map, carefully memorizing the key details.

This could go sideways very easily, she reminded herself.

Bob August's Residence, Spire

"Fuckwits!" he barked, standing in the doorway of his apartment.

Maya noticed a pulsing at his throat. She found herself genuinely concerned about his blood pressure. "Forty-five years of service," he ranted, "and they put me out on my ass like that!"

Paige glanced nervously up and down the corridor. "You wanna invite us in? I'm sure you don't want your neighbors to know—"

"Sod the damn neighbors. They can all know for all I care. In fact," he waved his finger like a warrior, "I want the world to know how they've treated me! And it's not just me, you know?" He wandered away from the door and disappeared into the apartment.

Maya looked at Paige with comically raised eyebrows. "So much for needing a delicate, covert approach," she teased as the pair took it as an invitation to follow him in.

They headed down the hallway into the living area which looked out onto the street four stories below.

Maya glanced at Paige, communicating intuitively that she would take the lead on the interview. Paige didn't need to do anything to confirm the move. "So, Bob, what happened?" Maya asked in her most soothing voice possible.

Bob was pouring a drink. He turned, waving his hands absently, still wired. "New exec team moved in, moved me out. Put some woman in my place."

Paige stifled a smile. She could tell it wasn't about her being female. There was something else going on.

"Who?" Maya pressed, back in investigative mode like a duck taking to water.

Bob took a swig of his whiskey and shook his head in dismay as he swallowed. "Some Rosaline Porter. Helviti knows who she is, though. Never heard of her on the circuit before she showed up at my office the day they told me the news."

Maya frowned. "So, she doesn't have any experience?"

"Don't think so. Unless she was a hot shot on Ogg, and we've just never heard of her."

Maya took a note on her holo. "Interesting," she muttered. "You heard anything about how things are being run there now?"

Bob started to simmer down. "Not really. They've gotten rid of a few of the guys, and everyone's obviously pissed about the change. Making them do weekly meetings, whether they're out in the field or what not. Plus, they've cut all funding for asset development."

Paige frowned at Maya questioningly.

"We had an allowance for hotels and paying informants when we were chasing a story," Maya explained. She paused. "You know, without that, it won't be long before there are no real stories to talk about. I mean, the investigative journalism department was already thin on the ground from the old days. That all but wipes it out."

Bob grunted something incoherent then coughed. "You're telling me! It's going to the dogs, that place. You mark my words."

He turned to pour himself another drink. Maya appeared next to him, took the bottle off him, and placed it gently back on the counter. "Hey, Bob, you know, there may be more to this than just a hostile takeover for money."

"What do you mean?"

"Well, I can't go into details, but we've found indicators to suggest there's something bigger going on here."

"Bigger? Like what?" His brow furrow turned from one of anger to one of serious contemplation. The editor in him seemed to reawaken to the scent of a story.

"Like..." Maya glanced furtively at Paige. Paige blinked slowly, giving her the go ahead. Maya continued. "Like, a larger agenda. I tracked the payments to Info Corp. I think there's a political move going on. What would help us narrow it down is to find out any specifics about what's changed in the news runs. You know, like what stories are being pushed from the top office. What stories are being shut down or relegated to fewer eyes. What changes are being made to the algorithms in the tech department. That kinda thing."

Bob listened intently. "I think I understand," he relayed slowly. He moved around the kitchen counter where he had an old-school pen and paper. He scribbled some notes. "There are a few people I can probably talk to." He hesitated. "Might take me a while. I'd need to do it on the down low… and take precautions."

Maya nodded gravely. "Of course. I know how it can get."

Bob raised his eyebrows at her. "I know you do," he said pointedly. "Which also means that if there is something going on, we need to be careful. You can't be seen down here again. We can set up some protocols so that I can feed what I find back to you, but no more direct contact." He looked at her sternly. "You shouldn't even be here today."

Maya smiled, once again feeling like the little girl that had wandered into his newsroom all those years ago, looking for a job. "I know," she admitted. "But… it's been so long, and…"

Bob stepped toward her and wrapped his arms around her. "I know," he said gently, holding her tightly.

Paige shifted her weight awkwardly, not wanting to spoil the moment but also not wanting to break it up by leaving.

Bob released Maya and held her at arm's length. "Look, kiddo, this hasn't been safe since the Jessica Newld fiasco. You don't wanna be caught up in whatever is going down here now, so promise me you'll get out of here and stay out of harm's way? I'll get you what I can, but you stay safe, agreed?"

Maya started to protest, but Bob silenced her with a glare. "I mean it, Maya. We didn't go through all that for you just to get picked off by one of these corporate hustles."

Maya nodded obediently. "Okay. I'll stay off-world unless I need to be here on a mission then."

That seemed to satisfy Bob. He looked over at Paige, still not releasing Maya from his hands. "You'll see to it?" he asked.

Paige nodded. "Yes, sir."

"Okay." He let go of Maya's shoulders. They firmed up their plan and how he would communicate, and within a matter of minutes, Paige and Maya were trotting quietly back down the stairs in silence, watching carefully all around them for any signs of being followed.

CHAPTER ELEVEN

The two suited Leath jogged heavily down the steps from the church, looking around to make sure they weren't being noticed. They exchanged a furtive glance and headed off to the right, away from the main drag and off into the undergrowth of the unkempt graveyard.

As they approached the rest of their team, they started to relax. Their boss, Ak'or, appeared from behind a large tombstone. He was smoking a beamy. He took the last puff as he saw them coming and then tossed the butt of it into the grass. "Well?" he grunted expectantly, looking them both up and down with a look of casual disdain.

"All good, boss," the first Leath reported.

"Yeah, all good," his partner confirmed.

"Signs of weapons?" the boss asked.

The first guy shook his head. "Nothing big, boss. The 'borgs are probably packing under their jackets, but we can take them out. No problem." He punched his large fist into his other hand with a thud. His heavy jaw jutted out, making him look even

133

more aggressive than his large build and bushy, overhanging eyebrows already did.

He glanced at the rest of his team unpacking their gear in the clearing of the simulated graveyard. Everything had to come on board through metal detectors, which meant that they were using carbon weapons which needed to be assembled. This was the only reason why they were setting up now and not sitting around, smoking and chewing the fat.

His gaze shifted nervously back to his boss. "Anything else you want us to do, boss?" he asked.

The commander's eyes looked dark with impulses of revenge. "No," he grunted roughly. "Just get set up. We'll move as soon as this ridiculous fiasco is over."

The flunkies nodded and moved off to join their buddies to prepare.

Meanwhile, a matter of yards away on the other side of the church, a group of five Noel-ni were doing the same thing. Having broken into the sim-deck from the upper floor and lowered themselves down on thin but intensely strong cable threads, they now assembled, quietly loading up their revolving tommy guns, waiting for the perfect opportunity to attack.

Each wore their traditional dress of a metal tunic that covered their humanoid torso. It was a matter of honor. This meant they had to stay agile and out of the way of any bullets, simply because they had so much exposed fur.

Brian, their leader, quietly barked the orders to the others. He pushed his damp nose in the air, sniffing the atmosphere for clues of who might be on the inside of the sim structure.

Being the pack leader, they were compelled to fall in line, regardless of their own thoughts or impulses. Barry, the second in command, paced on all fours, agitated and awaiting the go signal. Diana watched him, bemused.

· · ·

<u>Hangar Deck, Gaitune-67</u>

Paige was the first to hop out of the pod, closely followed by Maya.

"So, what's our next move?" Maya asked, automatically putting her hand on Paige's shoulder as she jumped down.

Paige grabbed her bag from the floor of the hovering pod. "I'm not entirely sure. It feels like we could do with some help from Oz in hacking the services at Info Corp. And the Northern Clan folks."

Maya pulled a face. "Yep. We're kinda screwed when Molly isn't about. Though…"

Paige had started walking across the hangar deck to the safehouse stairs. She turned back when she heard Maya hesitate. "What?"

"We have Bourne," Maya said slowly.

Paige pulled her lips to one side of her face. "Does he even know how to hack? And can he do it without setting off any alarms, or having it traced back to us?"

Maya opened her mouth to comment but was interrupted by a voice in her audio implant. It was Bourne's simulated voice. "Yeah, I can. You seem to be forgetting I escaped a military base when I was barely a few days old. And now, I've got all this intel on how the world works."

Maya was about to correct him and remind him that he was in fact rescued, but Paige shook her head, stopping her. "Oh, you've been studying?" Paige asked instead. She grinned at Maya, and they kept walking toward the safehouse.

"I have," Bourne boasted. "I watched a whole bunch of Mission Impossible, James Bond, Mr. Robot, and Chuck. I can do this."

Paige and Maya exchanged nervous glances.

Maya waved her hand casually, allowing Paige to continue with a response, glad now she hadn't gotten herself embroiled in the conversation with him.

Paige stumbled over her words. "Erm… right. This is totally awesome of you to volunteer, Bourne. Really appreciated. But… I'm thinking maybe we should wait until Molly gets back." She hesitated. "Just in case, you know, it's the wrong move and she wants us to… er, try another angle or something."

Bourne seemed perfectly relaxed about the response. "Yeah. Sure. Whatever. Just know, I'm ready to go at a moment's notice. I was *Bourne* ready!" he added enthusiastically.

Maya stopped walking and creased over, laughing silently. Paige rolled her eyes and leaned closer to whisper to Maya. "I blame the parents!"

Maya shook her head, mimicking Paige's tone. "He's a product of a misguided youth culture."

The pair sniggered quietly, careful not to be heard over the inbuilt intercom in their holos, which Bourne must have been tapped into.

"Okay, cool," Paige managed to say in a composed voice loudly so that Bourne would hear. "Thanks, Bourne. I appreciate it. We'll keep you posted."

Then she turned to Maya as they headed up the stairs. "Let's see what else we can do in terms of managing this health and safety issue. I'm thinking if we can get ahead of the points they'll be investigating, then we'll have a chance. If they can't find anything to shut us down for…"

"Then they can't shut us down," Maya finished.

"Exactly."

The pair strode through the door to the demon door corridor. "Okay," Maya agreed, pulling up another holoscreen and linking into the base's extended network as she walked. "I'll see if I can find a list of their inspection criteria."

Paige nodded. "Cool. Meet you in the base conference room shortly."

· · ·

<u>Level 40, Sim-deck 25, Glom Space station, Kirox Quadrant</u>

Having docked as close as they could to the sim-deck, the team headed down another docking corridor to find that the floor opened into what could only be described as an outdoor simulation.

The team traipsed into the third sim-deck they had examined since they docked.

How many others are there to check after this? Molly asked Oz mentally.

There are only another two that are running simulations right now. All the others are powered down.

Out of nearly a hundred of them? Odd they have all this unused capacity.

They probably get busier when there are gatherings happening. Or in the evenings.

I never did get that.

What? Their business model?

No. Evenings. I mean, on a space station, there's no night and day. Why bother?

Circadian rhythm? It's how most species operate.

No. But what keeps us doing it? Habit? Health? Why do we naturally save the drinking and partying until after a certain time, which on a space station is completely arbitrary.

Are you being derisive about your species' tendency to have an agreed social protocol related to time, which you all seem to abide by?

I guess I am.

Sometimes, I wonder who is more of the outsider: you or me. At least I try to fit in with cultural norms... now that I'm aware of them.

Ha! You trying to out-human me?

Maybe.

Hmm, something to prove, my inorganic friend?

"I can't believe this is real," Brock gasped, looking up at the simulated sky and trees and interrupting Molly's train of thought.

"Well, it's not," Crash pointed out dryly. "That's the point. You think those are trees? They're not. It's just your brain is being messed with by electromagnetic signals to make you think those are trees and sounds and birds and shit."

"Beats the seedy simulated bars and brothels we've just gate-crashed," Joel remarked, readjusting the blaster on his back as he glanced sideways at Crash. "Anyway, how come you know so much about this?"

Crash appeared suddenly flustered. "I erm… I used to come to a place like this. For fun."

Pieter glanced at Joel, who was also regarding Crash suspiciously. "Right then," Joel said, clearing his throat and changing the subject. "Despite this appearance of country lanes and fields, the plan of the physical place says we need to head in that direction and that there will be a building up ahead. That's where Sean is probably being held, according to Oz's interpretation of the layout."

Brock snorted as he checked his blaster and repositioned the bandolier of grenades he had around his torso. "Well, I'll take that with a pinch of salt. Seems Oz is just guessing right now."

"To be fair, he had nothing other than the layout to go off," Crash muttered to Brock, still recovering from the embarrassment of his confession. "Give the guy a break, eh? It's not like Sean is wearing a tracker."

Pieter closed the holoscreen he had been fiddling with, despite holding a pistol rather awkwardly in his other hand. "Yeah. No connection with his holo. The captors may have ditched it. Or turned it off."

"Oh, woah, check that out!" Joel called to the whole group. They looked up to see the simulated road they were walking on open up to display a church.

"That's it!" Brock exclaimed. His face turned from one of

delight at seeing the quaint building, to one of determination. "Let's go get those helvitis!"

Molly quickened her stride to catch up to the group. "Slow down, guys. We need a plan of approach. Who knows what we'll be walking into?"

The guys slowed their pace and turned to her for instructions. Jack had been casing the outer perimeter from a wide angle and quietly jogged up and joined them. "We've got company," she told them. "Just saw two meatheads come out of the front of the building."

Molly thought for a moment.

Oz? Any way to get a read on how many bodies are in the sim deck?

Afraid not. There are no heat sensors. And this was booked for a group event so people can come and go without registering for bandwidth.

Shit.

"Okay, so that's two that we know of," she clarified for the team. "No way of knowing how many others might be around, so we need to play this carefully."

Jack shifted her blaster on her hip. She too was loaded up on ammo and weapons. *Enough to take out a platoon of Federation grunts singlehandedly,* Joel thought as he noticed how she wasn't even out of breath from her brief reconnaissance mission.

"Okay," Molly said, opening her holo and drawing out a map of the terrain she could see ahead of them. "Here's the building. Here's the front. This is where those two goons came out." She glanced at Jack. "Which direction did they go?"

"They went off in this direction," Jack explained, pointing on the diagram and drawing in a line with her finger. "But I dunno if there's another building over there or what. There was some cover... bushes and stuff."

"Okay, anything else? Any other doors?"

Jack shook her head. "Not that I saw. I didn't go all the way around. I'd find it hard to believe they simulated it with just one entryway."

"Unless," Joel interjected, "they designed it to be a holding cell."

Molly clicked her fingers. "Good point." She shook her head. "This world... it's just nuts. That someone could simulate a holding cell out of brainwaves that would potentially keep someone trapped... incredible!"

Pieter nodded enthusiastically and started to interject.

Jack coughed. "Maybe we should marvel later and 'mission' now?"

"Right," Molly agreed. "So, I guess we can just all go in the front door then. Although Jack, do you think you could take care of those two that disappeared off that way? If they didn't come back down this lane, they probably weren't heading out of the sim."

Jack nodded. "Got it."

"Okay," Molly said, straightening up and grabbing the blaster off her back. "Let's lock and load."

She started striding out ahead of the group, closely followed by Brock, Crash, and Joel.

Pieter scurried after them, bringing up the rear, and Jack stalked back off into the undergrowth to take care of the two bogies who had already revealed themselves.

Joel and Crash took the lead and strode up the steps to the huge wooden doors of the apparent church.

"Go on three," Joel mouthed to Crash. "One, two, *three!*"

Crash and Joel barged through the doors, quickly followed by Pieter and Molly. Guns poised, ready to fire on anything that moved.

Only then did they realize that there had been a hubbub of

activity behind the doors, which suddenly silenced when they burst through.

"Oh crap," Joel muttered, lowering his weapon slowly, distracted by the scene ahead of them.

"Holy mongoose," Molly murmured.

Oz started laughing hysterically in Molly's head, tingling her spine annoyingly.

Oz, stop. For fuck's sake.

Molly looked out at the hundreds of faces turned in their direction, sitting in the sea of pews, dressed to the nines.

"Bride or groom?" a gruff-looking, suit-wearing cyborg asked them politely.

Brock slapped his leg several times, doubling over, laughing silently, and unable to respond.

Joel pushed past Crash and Brock to talk to the cyborg. "Sorry, what?"

"Are you from the bride's side or the groom's?" the usher clarified.

Joel's mouth hung agape. His eyes surveyed the faces that were still watching in rapt interest at the bizarre party that had just arrived, armed to the teeth.

Molly folded up her blaster and started to stow it away in the foyer. Crash followed suit, followed quickly by Pieter. Just at that moment, Jack came bounding in, blaster primed, ready to fire.

She stopped in her tracks.

Molly nodded at her folded-up blaster in the cloakroom area of the entranceway, pushed up against the coats. Jack looked completely confused and then powered hers down too and did the same.

Joel, meanwhile, had found his words. "I'm sorry I..." Then he spotted Sean down at the front of the church. His eyes nearly popped out of his head. "Sean?"

"The groom, then," the usher confirmed, making a cunning

deduction. "This way." He signaled to the right-hand side and indicated that the party should follow.

Brock managed to pick himself up off the floor where he had been recovering from his quiet laughing fit. Quickly, and still grinning, he started taking the grenades off his sash and putting them into pockets out of sight.

The cyborg usher showed them to a half-empty pew. Joel filed in first, followed by Molly, then Jack, Pieter, Crash, and finally Brock.

An old lady sat on the back bench on the bride's side. She appeared astounded and very interested in the bizarre newcomers. She caught Brock's eye as he sheepishly disarmed himself. He winked at her and continued grinning.

The rest of the congregation had restarted their chatter, and apart from the odd glance in their direction, Molly's team was mostly forgotten again.

Joel was looking around, trying to gather more clues as to what was going on. He saw Sean loitering around the front of the church, talking to people who approached him, shaking his hand and wishing him well.

"Sean's getting married?" he whispered in disbelief. "Is this real? Who's he marrying, even?"

Molly stood up. "I'm going to find out." She clambered over his long legs blocking her path to the other end of the row and then pushed her way past the other guests filling the pew. She staggered out onto the outer aisle.

Joel's gaze followed her. "Be careful," he hissed, still not entirely sure they should be putting their weapons away.

She flapped her arm at him in a manner that she obviously thought was discreet and strode off to the front.

CHAPTER TWELVE

<u>Level 40, Sim-deck 25, Glom Space station, Kirox Quadrant</u>

Molly strode down the side of the church, keeping her head down and trying to attract as little attention as possible.

She felt eyes all over her, watching her every move. Scrutinizing her. She did her best to ignore the attention. At least people were talking amongst themselves. Even if it *was* about the strange party who were probably gatecrashing the event.

Molly found her way to the front where Sean was waiting nervously. He turned to look at her. His expression of social discomfort turned to one of shock: like a child who had been caught with its hand in the cookie jar.

Molly's expression was now blank. She just stared at him in his full wedding outfit, stunned.

"I... Molly," he said, reaching out to touch her.

She took half a step back. "Is there somewhere we can talk?"

Sean composed himself. "Yeah. Erm... This way." He motioned toward a door a few yards back from where she had come and then led her in. It was clearly the groom's dressing room. There were discarded clothing packets and hangers hanging on bits of church furniture. On the dresser, there was a bottle of Yollin

Brandy and a few empty glasses. Her eyes clocked them and then turned to interrogate Sean.

"What the hell, Royale?" she blurted out, her composure evaporating in an instant.

He looked flustered. "Well, yeah. Would you believe me if I told you that it's not what it looks like?" He scratched the back of his head, pulling his suit into an awkward shape around his torso.

"You mean, it doesn't look like you've been kidnapped, and in order to orchestrate your release, you're having to get married?" she asked, her expression returning to blank.

He looked down at his feet, his hair disheveled now. "Ah. So. Erm, yeah. It's almost exactly what it looks like, then."

Molly stared at him incredulously. "What the fuck is going on?"

"You've gatecrashed my wedding!"

"Are you serious?"

"As a bullet in the head," he said grimly.

"Why?"

He shrugged. "Only way out of a tight situation."

"Come on. We have guns. We can get you out of here." She grabbed his sleeve and moved back toward the door, reaching for her pistol.

He moved and put his hand against the door, stopping her from opening it. Then he put his other hand on her pistol, stopping her from drawing it. "No," he said quietly. "The only way I'm leaving here is married."

Molly frowned, confused. "We can get you out of here. Easy. We just walk out. We're docked just down the hall."

He shook his head. "You don't understand. I can't. It's not just me."

Molly moved her hand from the door knob. "The bride?" she guessed.

He shuffled his feet. "Yeah, Karina," he confessed. "It's my fault she's in this mess. And she needs a fresh slate. This is the only way."

Molly retreated into the room so their voices wouldn't be heard. "What are you talking about? Grab her and we'll get her out, too."

His expression was one of a broken man, torn between worlds. "It's not that simple. If she runs, she'll never be free. We may as well shoot her now."

Molly reached again for the pistol strapped to her leg. "Okay," she said, starting toward the door.

"No!" He stopped her again. "It's complicated. And there isn't time to explain now. But I *do* have to do this."

Molly looked at him blankly, processing the options. Her mind came up with five different scenarios of how to extract both him and the bride. Not one of those scenarios explained why he would want to stay and go through with this legally binding ceremony… which *would* be binding, even if it was under duress.

Her mind raced, trying to comprehend what might have happened. "Has someone got something on you?" she tried again.

He shook his head, then stopped. "Well, yes. But not really. Look, it's complicated. But stay, and I'll explain everything later."

Molly took a deep breath.

Oz? What do I do?

It's Sean. You need to trust him.

But he's... getting married!

Which is his decision.

Can we do a tox screen? Maybe he's been drugged. What do we need? Blood sample? I can punch him and probably bust his lip—

Molly, *no!* He's showing no signs of drugs or doping.

How do you know?

I'm able to track things like heartbeat and pupil dilation and response times just watching him.

"Molly?" Sean pressed, his face gaunt and showing signs of fatigue.

"Yeah." Molly realized she'd been staring at him while having the Oz conversation. "Anything I can do?"

The tension in Sean's jaw seemed to relax a small amount. "Go get some good pictures. And tell those boys to stand down. No shooting today."

"Fine." She nodded abruptly and strode out of the room, leaving the door open.

Sean could tell she was upset.

She felt sore. Rejected. And guilty. Like this was her fault.

I just don't understand why he would want to do this.

We clearly don't have all the facts.

But I can't imagine a world where he would want to be doing this. We've never known him to even have a girlfriend. Or a relationship of any kind.

I know. We'll find out, I'm sure. We just need to make sure you get through the ceremony without causing a scene.

What makes you think I'd cause a scene?

Your heartrate is elevated. As are your cortisol levels. The last time I measured anything like this was in the Estarian safehouse when you'd just been rejected by Joel.

I was never rejected by Joel.

Well, technically... maybe not. But that's how your physiology interpreted it.

Well, fuck. Molly started in another direction.

Where are you going?

Restroom.

No. Keep it together. You need to be out here. We still don't know what's really going on.

The music started.

Get back to your seat. I'll see what I can do about getting your systems back to normal parameters so you can get through this.

Without causing a scene?

Yes. Without causing a scene. That is your mission.

Molly scowled. *Well, if this is a real wedding, at least there will be alcohol soon.*

Yes, focus on the positive. Wait! This pew.

Molly stopped in her tracks and backtracked to her pew. "I'm sorry, would you excuse me?" she asked politely to the Zyhn-like creature on the end.

She pointed to her party. The person stepped out and allowed her to pass, and the Yollin sitting next to him pressed himself back so she could squeeze past him, too. She shuffled her way along the row, bypassing the guests to end up back with the others.

She plonked herself down next to Joel. "Everything okay?" he asked.

Molly looked straight ahead. "Apart from feeling completely underdressed and overarmed, yes. Oh yeah, and Sean wants us to trust him and let him go through with this."

"Any explanation?" Joel asked.

She shook her head slightly, looking down at a program she had picked up from the ledge in front of her. "Nope. He said he'll explain later."

"Well, I guess we can only follow his lead. He's probably on an op."

"Let's hope so," Molly agreed. "Otherwise, this is just too confusing."

Just then, everyone stood up and turned to see the bride coming down the aisle.

Molly hauled herself to her feet, too, and turned to look, craning her neck. She couldn't see.

Joel saw her struggling to catch a glimpse and turned toward her. "Don't worry, she's not even that pretty," he said, half teasing her, half trying to comfort her.

Molly looked up at him, locking eyes. She couldn't understand why she hurt so much. But somehow, Joel seemed to know exactly what she was going through. He put his arm around her and pulled her close as he pretended to pay attention to what was going on ahead of them now.

The crowd hushed and the music stopped.

"Dearly beloved, we are gathered here today…" a voice boomed through the simulated building.

"Oh, my ancestors!" Brock hissed past Crash to Pieter.

Pieter looked concerned. "What is it?" His eyes darted nervously around the crowd ahead of him, looking for the threat.

"I love her shawl!" Brock exclaimed as discreetly as he could.

Pieter relaxed, noticing out of the corner of his eye that even Crash smirked.

Pieter craned his neck to see where Brock was looking. "Oh, the shimmery one?"

"Yeah."

Pieter smiled to himself. Brock continued to eye the crowd, presumably out of his interest in the fashion more than staying sharp for possible problems.

"Yeah," Pieter continued, sitting down so their conversation would be less conspicuous while everyone else stood and listened to the priest. Brock did the same. "I hear they've started making those shawls with the guts of abbey worms. Apparently, they are only found on exoplanets with enough sulfur in the atmosphere."

Brock frowned and looked at Pieter now. "How the heck do they harvest them, then?"

"In space suits. And using lots and lots of Teshovians, I heard."

Someone behind them coughed, trying to get them to be quiet.

"No way!" Brock exclaimed, glimpsing the angry glare from the people behind and trying to lower his voice even more.

"Yeah. It's a big business in the fashion industry. At least, that's what Paige was telling me." Pieter slouched back in the pew.

"Fascinating."

"Yeah," Pieter agreed. "And Paige is going to be pissed that she's missing—"

"Oh, lordy," Brock interjected. "Look at those shoes!"

Crash and Pieter sat up and strained to see around the people gathering in the aisle where Brock was looking.

"I didn't know they made such glamorous stuff for Krenlock," Brock exclaimed.

The tall, scaly Krenlock must have overheard them because she turned and glared at them from her seat in a pew three rows in front of them.

Brock clamped a hand over his mouth. "Oops!"

Pieter shook his head. "You and your big mouth."

Brock sniggered. "Her and her big feet!" He noticed Crash's chest bouncing as he laughed silently between the two of them. "They must be a special line. Or a knockoff or something." Brock sniggered.

Crash made a very quiet sound, like the meow of a cat.

Pieter giggled and reached across Crash to slap Brock's arm. "Stop already! You're going to get us killed!" He peered between the standing people in front of them to see if he could still see the Krenlock. "And I don't know what her species normally looks like, but right now, she looks damn angry."

Brock sighed. "You're right," Brock agreed. "But you know, I don't think I've ever been in a room with so many different species. And that's saying something!"

"Yeah, I can believe that, mister free-love." Pieter chuckled.

Brock's smile faded. "You know, there's something else. Something I just can't put my finger on."

"Something wrong?" Crash asked.

"Yeah. It's… maybe it's just cause it's a sim. And bizarre circumstances…"

Crash spoke even more quietly now, keeping his face straight. "You're not thinking it's your grindle senses tingling?"

Brock tipped his head from side to side. "Maybe."

Pieter leaned back in the pew and then shifted awkwardly. "You know, now that you mention it, I got a funny feeling about all this, too. It's like there is something obvious staring us in the face, but we're not seeing it."

Brock sighed. "Yeah, I agree," he said, continuing his scan of the crowd around them.

Level 40, Sim-deck 25, Glom Space station, Kirox Quadrant

Jack listened attentively as the priest talked at the congregation. She noticed that on the bride's side, a stocky but older gentleman sat wiping his eyes and sniffing. She guessed he must be the father of the bride. She scanned for a woman of a similar age and noticed there wasn't anyone that fit the bill for the mother.

She became aware of someone behind her and a low whisper. She turned her head to catch, out of the corner of her eye, a rather tall, scaly creature leaning over to her. He looked like he expected an answer.

"I'm sorry?" Jack whispered back, turning a little more to regard him carefully. "Did you…"

He nodded. "Yes," he said, in a guttural-sounding accent. "I was admiring your piece."

Jack glanced down at her chest, then realized he was signaling at the butt of her pistol shoved into her holster under her arm. "Oh!" she mouthed, trying to brighten her face and look social rather than mission-focused. "Thank you!" she mouthed. "Custom," she added, trying to be polite.

The creature looked at her approvingly and then went back to listening to the ceremony.

Jack turned and saw Brock sniggering quietly to himself on the end.

Crash jabbed him gently in the ribs, trying to get him to behave. He looked right and caught Pieter's eye. Pieter smiled, clearly amused by the pair. Crash rolled his eyes and sighed, like it pained him to have to be the only grown up.

Pieter deduced that Crash was still getting used to the relationship thing, considering that the facial expression was probably the most expression he'd seen out of Crash in a social situation… ever.

Brock was distracted again, now communicating silently with hand gestures with an old dear over on the other side of the aisle. She was pointing at his crotch. Brock was trying to figure out what she was getting at. And then he realized it was his pockets. He pulled out the grenade that was causing the rather obvious bulge. She turned her finger, asking him to turn it over. He obliged. She squinted and then straightened up and gave him a thumbs-up. He replaced it in his pocket. Then, she whispered loudly across to him. "I use those when I can get my hands on them. Hard to find in stock round here, though."

"Shh!" Several people all at once turned around and shushed her.

She glared in the direction of one of them and stared down the back of his head before looking back at Brock for moral support. Brock tried to suppress his smile and pretended to be listening to the priest again.

He hadn't been quiet for more than thirty seconds before he leaned over to Crash next to him. "Paige and Maya are going to be pissed they missed the chance to dress up," he whispered as quietly as he could.

Crash nodded without taking his eyes from the front.

"And being bride's maids!" Crash added. "Yeah. That's huge. Sean's in for it… if he survives this."

He was quiet for a moment.

"You think there is a reception afterward?" Brock hissed again.

Crash shrugged.

"Okay, I'll shut up and let you watch Sean's fake wedding in a fake church."

Crash turned and locked eyes with Brock. "You think it's fake?" he asked in a really low voice, his lips moving as much as a ventriloquist's.

Brock shrugged. "He goes missing, and then we find him getting hitched to some chick we've never heard of? It's either a ruse or an escape plan."

Crash reacted with his eyes before turning back to the front. "Ironic escape plan," he mused.

Brock was quiet again for about ten seconds. "You saying that marriage is a prison? Or a hostage situation?"

Crash almost inceptively sighed with frustration. "No. I wasn't saying that. I was talking about this situation."

He could tell Brock was extrapolating to his views in general. He gently inched his foot closer to Brock and shifted closer to make arm to arm contact.

Brock relaxed, feeling suddenly reassured.

The service had been going for a good half hour. The priest had talked about the nature of love and the commitment that the happy couple were making to each other.

Molly felt like her brain was going to implode.

"So, if anyone here has any reason why these two people should not be joined in holy matrimony, speak now, or forever hold your peace."

Molly felt a wave of adrenaline hit her.

I could...

Don't even think about it.

She raised her eyes to look up at the front and noticed that there was a lot of attention in her direction. It took her another moment to realize that the entire team was looking directly at her.

And the people all around her were looking to her and her team, as if that was why they were here.

Well, she thought, *it is exactly why we're here.*

Don't.

Molly glanced over at the others. Joel, Jack, Crash, Pieter, and Brock. Every single one of them looked at her expectantly.

Was her silence letting the team down?

Should she be fighting for Sean, even though he had told her not to?

"What?" she hissed at them angrily.

"Nothing," Brock whispered, snapping his eyes back to the front like a soldier. All the others did the same.

The priest was looking in their direction, too. Molly felt her face flush. Then, she saw Sean turn around to glare at her.

She felt mortified. Like she just wanted the ground to open up and swallow her down every deck and into empty space.

She caught her breath and looked down, studying her fingernails as hard as she could, waiting for the burning gazes to turn their attention away from her. She felt her whole body overheat.

Glancing up to see if the ceremony was continuing, she saw that the priest was still looking at her, as if giving her one last opportunity to not have to hold her peace for all eternity.

The bodies in the church shifted impatiently, some straining to see what they were all waiting for.

Her heart throbbed. She felt helpless and tearful. But she knew she couldn't react. She made eye contact with the priest and waved her hand as if to say she was waving her right.

Her last chance to understand what was going on.

The priest seemed to shrug, as if to say, "Don't say I didn't give you a chance." And then he continued.

Molly felt a piece of herself die. A part of her would never accept that this wasn't real. No matter how long this farce went on for. But maybe that was what she had to learn. To accept a reality, even when she knew in her bones that there was something wrong with it.

And maybe there ultimately was nothing wrong with it.

People made bad decisions all the time. And they went on living and breathing in some instances. There was always the next thing. The next chapter. And so it would be with Sean. Even if she didn't know what that looked like.

Even if it meant him leaving the team and her never seeing him again. At least it had been his decision, and she was in no way going against his wishes.

At least she had that.

A single tear trickled down her face before she discreetly knocked it away with the back of her finger.

CHAPTER THIRTEEN

Level 40, Sim-deck 25, Glom Space station, Kirox Quadrant

Pieter had been distracted throughout the ceremony.

There was another long reading happening, but by the old guy that was announced as the father of the bride. They were all standing for it. He wished he could just sit down. It wasn't a matter of fitness. It was like some boredom switch had been flicked on and his body just felt exhausted.

His eyes scanned the congregation for the zillionth time. Still, he couldn't shake the feeling that something was off. He looked to his left and across the aisle. It was definitely something about her side of the family that was bugging him. Apart from there being many more of them on that side...

And in the chatter beforehand, he noticed that some people who knew the other side were put on this side.

That would figure, he thought to himself. *I bet Sean doesn't have many people who he'd invite from his side. They must have run out of space on the bride's side.*

He noticed that they all seemed a certain type. Despite there being many different species in the room, it was as if they all belonged to the same tribe. Or family.

He narrowed his eyes, wracking his brain for what else he had noticed unconsciously. He noticed toward the back, there were lots of human cyborgs. Like a small contingent. An army. He watched them for a few moments until one of them noticed, and Pieter looked back at the front of the room.

A family. With their own personal army.

Where had he seen that before? he wondered.

Well, obviously in the mafia movies on the archives... Shit! That was it. That was why Sean was going through with it! He must have gotten caught up in a mafia thing on this mission, and now, he's deep undercover and...

His eyes were wide, and Brock must have noticed. He was looking over at him, demanding a silent explanation.

Pieter looked furtively around, trying to find some way to warn the others without drawing attention to themselves.

His mind raced.

The priest made his final proclamation. "You may now kiss the bride."

Sean leaned in and kissed the girl in the white dress, and applause erupted in the church. The father of the bride was beside himself with what Molly could only assume was happiness. Except he was crying and waving his hands.

Molly glanced over at Joel. "Well, I guess that's that," she said, as detached as if she'd been commenting on the weather. Joel started to say something comforting to her, but all of a sudden, there was a big bang at the back of the church, and people started screaming and shouting.

Then, there was a hail of bullets flying through the length of the simulated building.

Molly instinctively ducked and turned around.

I bet those aren't simulated bullets!

No such luck.

Panic erupted in the ranks of guests. People were scattering everywhere, shouting and squealing. "We've got company," she shouted down the pew to the others, who had already ducked for cover and were reaching for their weapons.

She peeked up over her pew to see a band of Leath brandishing tommy guns and firing into the crowd.

The bank of cyborgs at the back of the church seemed completely underprepared. They reached for their tiny pistols that they had concealed in their ankle holsters. Molly didn't have time to wonder why they had small guns and not something bigger in their jackets. They seemed like the type.

She had already pulled her guns from the holsters and scrambled out to the side aisle, keeping as low as she could so as not to get hit.

Not that they'd kill instantly. They look like lower caliber old-fashioned weapons.

They'd still do some serious damage. Could kill you if you take a bullet to the head. Or a vital organ. I'd advise against getting hit.

Thanks, Oz. I'll keep that in mind.

She carefully stalked down the aisle until she was only a couple of pews from the back. Then she started picking off the Leath, glad of the Jean Dukes she had to get the job done.

She took out two of the five in the first round but instantly drew the fire of the other three, who had already pushed the team of cyborgs into a side room to take cover.

Just then, there was shooting behind her. Quickly, she pivoted in her crouched position to see a few of the cyborgs were dealing with a threat of Noel-ni coming in from one of the back rooms. The fox-like humanoid creatures seemed to be using swords with a special forcefield that they used to deflect the bullets. They weren't firing any of their own. In fact, the swords also seemed to double as an actual sword. She watched as one of the cyborgs got within swords-length of one of them. The weapon cut straight through him like it was slicing through butter.

Motherfucker!

She noticed that Joel and Crash were firing at the remaining Leath. Brock was readying a grenade. Jack... she couldn't see where Jack was. But Pieter was safe with Joel.

She turned back to the front. Most of the guests had either scampered away or were taking cover between the pews.

There was only one thing for it: she was going to have to deal with the Noel-ni herself.

Keeping low, she stalked toward the front. She saw one had his sword raised above his head, about to bring it down on someone. Shit! It was the father of the bride. He cowered, petrified, one hand shielding his head. Molly stood briefly, firing off three shots, and watched the sword-wielding tyrant stagger back before falling over.

One of his comrades noticed. She was female. She turned, screaming, and ran toward the slumping body. In doing so, she forgot to shield herself, and a bullet blast whistled through and took her out.

Molly glanced to see where the other shot had come from and glimpsed Jack taking cover again.

All of a sudden, she felt movement behind her. A Noel-ni was coming at her with a sword, wielding it like a machete. She turned her body around and managed to fire with one pistol as she pivoted. It caught him in the gut, and though he was jumping through the air and the momentum was carrying him and his sword, she was just able to get out of the way of the sharp blade. The body of the dying Noel-ni knocked her to the ground, crushing the air out of her lungs as they both fell backward.

She could hear the guns firing and the continued kerfuffle of the war zone around her. She struggled to get the creature off her. He was heavy. And bleeding.

Ick.

Better ick than dead.

She sighed, trying to catch her breath so she could move

again. After a few moments, she tried again, and this time managed to get herself out from underneath the body.

That is… ugh.

The hail of bullets had stopped. A strange quiet, punctuated by groans and whispers, filled the church. Molly carefully surveyed the scene. She could see wedding guests hiding, some peeking to see if it was over. The bride was by her father's side, helping him up. Sean was standing over a Noel-ni. She could tell from his position that he'd gone up behind it and killed it with his bare hands. She shook her head, amused that even without a blaster, he was a deadly weapon.

Joel. Where was Joel? She panicked.

She scanned the area of the pews where he had been. Brock was the first to sit up on the bench. He was grinning, relieved and exhausted. Jack appeared from the other side of the room. Molly headed back up the outside aisle to check on the others. As she approached, Crash and Joel stood up. And then Pieter hauled himself up.

She wandered through a row to the center aisle. "Well, maybe we weren't that over-armed," she called over to Joel, who just burst out laughing.

It took a while for the guests to compose themselves, and then for station security to show up and start helping people out and taking statements. It took another half an hour or more for everything to be resolved and the bodies to be taken away.

"Well, it's a Sean Royale thing," Joel was saying to the group of Sean, the bride, and her father.

Sean looked confused.

"What?" Joel continued. "You didn't expect that Royale could have any kind of celebration or event without it involving a gunfight for good measure. Whole thing seems kinda apt to me!"

The group laughed hysterically, and Sean slapped Joel on the back. Molly watched carefully as she approached, not really sure she was ready to meet this strange bride that had convinced Sean to cut them off, risk his life, and then tie the knot.

Sean beckoned her over, and she walked more purposefully. "I was just introducing Joel to my wife and my father-in-law."

"Please, call me Dad!" Vito exclaimed.

"Okay… Dad!" Sean said, clearly embarrassed by the whole thing.

Sean presented Karina. "Karina, this is Molly Bates. Molly, meet Karina Royale. AKA Mrs. Sean."

Molly stepped forward to shake her hand. Karina, still clearly high on adrenaline from the gunfight, flung her arms around Molly. "Molly. So glad you could make the wedding!"

Molly tried to pull herself away from the smothering embrace and was about to protest about Sean being in mortal danger and how she hadn't been invited but was more trying to save his hide… when Joel put a hand on her shoulder and shook his head.

Molly relented and relaxed, allowing the girl to hug her. Slowly, she made an effort and put her hands on Karina's back. Sean caught her eye. He was clearly amused by the interaction.

Molly peeled herself away. "Well, congratulations, Sean," she said, holding out a hand to shake. "Glad you're not dead."

Sean knocked her hand away and hugged her.

Molly sighed, resigning herself to the new reality that at least during this damn wedding, she was going to be hugged.

"Very nice to meet you," the father of the bride said, stepping forward. "My name is Calzone. Vito Calzone."

Molly felt a mild relief as he pushed out his hand, rather than forcing her into a hug. "I must say," he continued in his strange accent, hardly opening his mouth as he talked, making the tone kind of suppressed and mumbled. "I'm very grateful that you and your friends were here with weapons." He glanced at Sean. "You know, all guests were instructed they weren't to bring weapons.

Just the family employees were meant to have a few guns, just in case."

Molly rolled her lips inward, wondering whether she should come clean. "We didn't get an invitation," she confessed. She glanced at Sean for backup.

Sean laughed heartily. "Yep, that's Molly. Just always showing up... uninvited!" He seemed nervous but moved toward her and slapped her on the back. Vito was laughing, too. Seeing *that*, Sean relaxed again, only to catch a scowl from his new bride, who was less than happy about him touching the leggy blonde who had happened to save all their lives.

"Well," Vito chuckled, "this party isn't going to start itself. Molly, I thank you for saving the wedding guests, myself, and my precious daughter. You are, of course, invited to the reception."

He raised his voice so that those around would hear him. "Time to move to the reception, people. This is a day of celebration, and we won't allow a little skirmish with rival families to interfere. Everyone to the One2One Bar on the main concourse of this level. Let the station staff finish clearing up the bodies in peace."

He waddled forward, disrupting the circle of people who were gathered in the group.

Molly and Joel folded away their weapons and followed. "I still feel underdressed, though," Molly murmured to Joel as they made their way out of the simulated church.

Wellness Spa, Aboard *The ArchAngel*, Sark System

The server in the spa area deposited two more martinis on the table between the two women and cleared away the empty ones.

Barb didn't want another martini but knew it was important to keep up with Carol. "So, what exactly did you do?"

Carol picked up the fresh martini. "I just had some of my

team put out some feelers. But of course, they had some kind of firewall in play and we got made."

"So, what happened?"

"Nothing." Carol shrugged. "Molly didn't even call."

Barb laid back and relaxed, closing her eyes. "Interesting. Did she know it was you?"

"I guess probably not," Carol confessed. "Else she would have been in touch. Or, at least, descended on our decoy facility."

Barb smiled. "I don't think she would have been fooled by a decoy facility."

"What makes you so sure? We have the best techs in the system."

"Oh, she has a pretty good team. And a good head on her shoulders." Barb smirked underneath her martini glass as she took another sip. "So, come on, what's going on? Why is your husband kidnapping you if all you're doing is putting out feelers for your daughter?"

Carol sighed, sitting up on the lounger and swinging her feet onto the floor. "Well," she confessed, "I might have overstepped."

"Overstepped how?"

"Well, I may have arranged for one of my ex-agents to make sure that my daughter and Sean Royale could never be involved… personally."

"How did you do that?"

"I, erm… I sent this agent to ensnare Royale. Take him out, as it were."

"You're kidding? Carol, you don't need me to tell you that that is insane, do you?" Barb looked perplexed, like she couldn't tell if she was talking to someone who was just driven or clinically insane.

Carol bobbed her head deferentially. "Well, it may have been a little rash," she admitted, as if she was confessing to having raised her voice in a meeting. "But I was emotional. And I haven't seen her for so long, and she acts like she's not my little girl anymore."

"So, you decide to interfere with someone else's life like that?"

"Well, technically, two someone elses' lives. But I don't want that rogue anywhere near her… with his cyborg enhancements and goodness knows what."

Barb sighed, ignoring the potential for a double entendre. "You know Sean is a good guy."

"Good guy my ass!" Carol scoffed, reaching for her drink again as if to medicate her anger. "He just uses women and then discards them. One after another."

"What makes you say that?"

"I've been keeping tabs on him. And besides, how do you think I came to have an agent from outside Estaria?"

"Sean?"

"Yup. Goodness knows where he found her, but he wiped her background and deposited her with Lance, who then put her through the academy and then pulled some strings to get her into my agency. Which is where she stayed until she retired five years ago."

"And what brought her out of retirement?"

"Me."

Barb shook her head. "I'm going to need another drink," she muttered and lifted her still half-full martini glass to the waiter.

Barb had directed the conversation off into other areas, deliberately getting Carol to open up about other things before steering their focus back to the problem at hand. Carol, however, was the one to change the subject back to Molly.

"So, do you have any idea what's going on?" she asked Barb, now slightly slurring her words. "Is the Federation in touch with my daughter?"

Barb frowned. "Lemme look," she said, opening her holo device and scrolling. "Oh, here we go. Yes, ADAM is monitoring the whereabouts of their ship, and the local news stations and security reports." Her eyes darted around the projected holographic screen for a few moments. "Hmm, it looks like…"

"What?" Carol pressed.

"Well, it seems there was a disturbance on a space station where a girl was kidnapped from. Here, they have an image."

Barb showed Carol the image of Karina going into the restaurant.

Carol slammed her hand over her mouth.

"Your operative?"

Carol nodded, keeping her hand in place.

Barb carried on flicking through the screen's data. "Ah… and some more. There was an attack with guns on a simulation deck on a trading outpost. There have been a few arrests, but most of the perpetrators were killed."

Carol seemed to quickly sober up. "Can we get an ID on any of them?"

Barb flicked some more. She shook her head. "Nope. They haven't been processed yet."

Carol put her hands over her face. "It's all my fault," she muttered from behind her hand, tears welling in her eyes.

Barb glanced over at her. "No, no, no. Hold on. We don't know that was Molly and her team. For all we know, she was the one doing all the killing. In fact, knowing what I do about that Sanguine Squadron, it probably *was* them. And look, ADAM updates this report every five seconds. We'll know more soon, I'm sure."

Carol tried to compose herself, but instead, she broke down.

Barb patiently consoled her, reaching across to touch her arm. "Come on, it's going to be okay. Molly knows what she's doing. And if Sean is still around, then they'll be back here in no time. I'm sure of it."

"I'm a terrible mother!" Carol howled through her hands.

Barb sat up and faced her, putting a hand on her shoulder.

"Now, now… You're not. Molly's turned out great. She's made the Federation proud on several occasions, and if anyone can deal with this mission, she can."

"I know, but I put her in this situation!" Carol insisted.

"Yes," Barb agreed. "You did. But the good news is you can help get her out of it."

Carol paused her sobbing and looked up at Barb. "How do you mean?"

Barb shrugged, clearly in control of the situation. "Well, you could start by explaining everything you know about this operative and what her play was. Then sharing all the intel you've gathered in your investigation would go a long way toward helping us help Molly get out of there safely."

Carol nodded, gulping her sobs back. "Yes. Anything. I'll do anything."

Barb signaled to the server. "We're going to need some coffee over here when you're ready," she said.

The server nodded and headed off to fill the order.

CHAPTER FOURTEEN

<u>Level 40, Sim-deck 25, Glom Space station, Kirox Quadrant</u>

The party was just leaving the church when Karina suddenly piped up. "Daddy! I need to throw the bouquet!"

"Oh, of course," he gasped. "See who the next lucky lady is to get hitched." He winked at Sean, who tried to maintain a polite expression. He thought about warning the others not to play the game, but then figured that Vito couldn't exactly go around insisting that random couples get married.

Vito shuffled everyone around and down the steps, leaving Karina standing at the top, pleased as punch. Station staff scuttled by with a gurney with a black body bag on top and adeptly navigated their way down the steps and out of the way of the guests.

Molly's crew and the remaining wedding guests assembled obediently. Molly deliberately stood at the back, out of the way and ready to leave for the bar. The idea of a proper drink was increasingly appealing with each social interaction she suffered through.

"On three!" Vito called, waving a stick as if conducting an orchestra. "Everybody count! Big throw Karina, dear!"

Karina turned around, bouquet in hand, and began winding up to toss it behind her.

The crowd counted with increasing hope and enthusiasm.

"One."

"Two."

"Three!" The bouquet left Karina's hands and flew up into the air. It had height rather than distance, Molly noted. This meant it would come down right in the middle of the crowd.

There were squeals of delight. Dozens of female hands went up into the air, reaching for the symbolic bunch of flowers that held bizarre magical prophecies of them bagging a mate.

Molly smiled, watching.

Joel nudged her. Molly glanced briefly at him, taking her eyes off the crowd for a split second. Joel was looking in the direction of the bouquet. Molly followed his gaze.

Fuuuuuuuck!

It was coming straight for her. She moved to shield her face, having only an instant to make a move before it would hit her in the face. Her hands went up and without thinking about the repercussions, she caught it.

The crowd erupted in a cheer. Joel threw his arm around her, amused at her reaction. Molly stood, mouth agape and cheeks beet red.

Her eyes met with Karina's. Karina seemed quite satisfied with herself. Molly wasn't sure why.

Then, she also noticed three or four of the ladies, including the Krenlock, glaring at her, unamused. Everyone else seemed quite pleased with the result. It probably helped that Joel was right next to her and the obvious candidate for a match.

Molly, unsure of quite what she should do, waved to Karina and tried to thank her with a thumbs-up. Then she shoved the flowers into Joel's arms and started walking out of the sim deck.

She needed a drink.

And she hoped to hell this wasn't a real mission, or else she'd be forced to stay sober and alert. Only another conversation with Sean would determine that. She glanced behind her to see him with his bride and the crowd breaking up and heading to the door, too. Joel was talking with Jack and Pieter, showing them the flowers.

She shook her head and strode toward the exit. If she couldn't get a drink straight away, at least she could remove herself from this nightmare of a social occasion.

Lance's Office, Aboard *The ArchAngel*, Sark System

Barb sat next to Carol, one arm around her back, consoling her as the shell of a director for clandestine services sobbed quietly into a tissue.

"I made a horrible mistake," she confessed. Philip stood on the other side of the room, more of an observer than a participant in the conversation.

Lance poured her another drink and handed it to her. Barb took it from him and placed it on the table, well aware that the last thing Carol needed was more alcohol in her system.

"We need to find Molly," Carol continued.

Lance rocked on his heels. "Oh, we know exactly where Molly is," he revealed.

Carol looked up confused. "How come?"

"Carol," Lance said firmly, without a hint of condescension, "this is the Federation. And I can't let you in on the details of our tech. You're a foreign government. But we've pinpointed the exact space station, and we're making arrangements to speak with her directly. I can assure you she's safe. For now."

"For now?" Philip interjected.

"Yes, for now," he replied. He turned back to Carol. "You were right about your daughter being in danger. Just wrong about the location of the danger. ADAM analyzed the data you turned over. It seems that our suspicions are correct. There are indeed threats brewing in your own backyard… without you needing to send her off into the middle of a mob wedding."

"A mob wedding?" Carol interrupted.

"Yes. Seems that's why she's been unreachable."

"Not hers I hope?" Carol asked, her eyes wide with alarm.

"No, no," Lance confirmed. "She's attending one as I hear it. Hence the shootout."

"How can you know that?" Carol asked. "You can't possibly be receiving intel over those distances. They haven't been gone a few days. How can you know what she's doing right now?"

Lance smiled. "Like I said, tech-knowledgy. And the how is on a need-to-know basis only." He chuckled to himself and looked to Philip for support. "Get it. Knowledge. Tech—Oh, never mind."

"But she's safe?" Carol pressed.

"Yes, she's safe. They've got everything under control."

Philip interjected again. "So, what about this trouble brewing in our own backyard?"

Lance took a deep breath and wandered around to his console chair at his desk. "Well, the chatter is indicating that there are people maneuvering into certain positions of power in order to create some kind of movement on the government. Have you ever heard of the Northern Clan of Cambodian?"

"No," Philip responded promptly.

Lance looked to Carol. She shook her head. "No, me neither."

"Well, you might wanna get eyes on them. They've moved three of their people into key military positions in the last twelve months, and now, we've noticed an influx of funds into the markets." He paused. "You remember the Newstainment takeover?"

"Yes, but that was legit," Carol countered, clearly confused by the unrelated events.

"It was," Lance agreed. "But it's still looking like someone is going to want to be controlling military and media. Something is coming, Carol. And you folks aren't ready."

Philip noticed how Carol didn't react to the statement, which would normally have made her react defensively. "What do we need in order to be ready?" she asked instead.

"Us," Lance said flatly. "Or more specifically, your daughter. You are aware that she has been training the planet's brightest and best to be ambassadors to protect your way of life?"

"Well, I was—"

Lance kept talking. "She's got an approach, and we just need to extend the approach to get these bright young things into positions where they can protect your citizens from what could be an impending tyranny."

"Are there any specific threats? I can have a team on it—"

Lance had been fiddling with a cigar on his desk. He tossed it down in front of him and leaned back in his seat. "Getting a team on it isn't going to help. This is *cyb-illa* warfare."

"Cybilla?" Carol queried, wiping one side of her face and under her eyes for any residue of tears.

"Yeah, it's cyber and guerilla, and it's happening right under your noses."

ADAM's voice connected through Lance's implant. "Sir, we have an incoming call request from Molly. Would you like to take it here? Or in your private office?"

Lance raised one finger to his guests. "Folks, Molly is making contact. I need to take this call. I'm going to try and get her up to speed so she's got time to process this on the way back."

The others watched and nodded.

Lance rocked back in his chair. "Okay, ADAM. Let's take the call here."

A holoscreen opened from his desk console, revealing an image of Molly looking somewhat worse for wear.

· · ·

Capitol Building, Spire, Estaria

Commander Richard Ekks placed his parade hat on the desk and sat down at his console in his new office. It was a pleasant relief to finally be able to close the door and mellow in the peace and quiet.

The day had been filled first with a parade ceremony in his honor and then a series of meetings and introductions, followed up with back slapping at the Senate.

He leaned back in his anti-grav chair.

I could get used to this, he thought, swiveling around and taking in the view of Spire from the tenth floor of the government building. He rocked himself gently for a few minutes, appreciating the moment.

Then, his holo chirped. It was an incoming call. He hit receive and sat up.

"Congratulations, Commander!" It was Raj Ghetti. He looked like he was on a space station somewhere. Richard never quite knew where Raj worked out of. He always seemed to be in transit or visiting somewhere. He'd spoken of an office on Ogg once, but Richard suspected it was for show.

"Mr. Ghetti, what a wonderful surprise!" Richard replied.

"How are you finding life as a commander of the Estarian-Ogg Space Fleet?"

"I'm liking it very much, sir. And I know it's in no small part thanks to you and your group. I must extend my sincerest gratitude for everything you've done to get me here."

Raj waved his hand. "You're welcome. But don't thank me yet. This isn't a free lunch."

"Of course, sir. I'm just honored to have the opportunity."

Raj smiled enigmatically. "Good. Well, I'll be in town in a few days. We should do lunch, and I'll fill you in with some details which will interest you very much."

"Oh?"

"Yes. This isn't a secure line, and, of course, it's of a sensitive nature."

"Of course," Richard agreed politely. "I understand."

"Good. Well, I'll have my people contact your people and we'll set it up."

"I'll look forward to it, sir."

"Excellent. And congratulations again, Commander."

"Thank you, sir."

Ghetti ended the call and the screen went blank. Richard sat once again in the quiet, pleased as punch that he had this new position. Somewhere in the back of his mind, he had a niggling feeling that the price tag it came with was much higher than he'd originally been led to believe.

He shook the thought from his consciousness and turned his attention to some messages he needed to respond to.

CHAPTER FIFTEEN

<u>Entertainment Deck, Bronislovas Trading Outpost, Kirox Quadrant</u>

The music had already begun.

At least, Molly assumed it was music. She wasn't sure if it was of a Yollin influence or something entirely different she had never even heard of. All she knew was that some of the guests who had already started drinking were bopping away to it from their chairs. It wouldn't be long until the dance floor in the center of the room would be filled with inebriated guests.

Her eyes scanned the scene, straining to make out Sean from amongst the numerous human and cyborg faces. Her eyes fought against the flashing lights and decorative lasers. She could feel the frustration rising in her chest.

Where the fuck is he?

I suspect he'll be along shortly if he's not already here.

As if on cue, there was a commotion behind her as cheering guests entered with Sean and his bride in their midst.

Molly rolled her eyes. It was bizarre to see Royale playing this part. She waited by the side as the rest of the party arrived, took pictures, and did the necessary convention of handshakes and what-have-yous. She noticed Joel and the others congratulated him and then headed into the party. Only Jack hung back, made eye contact with Molly, and then disappeared out of the door again.

I'm guessing she's staying alert to any other threats.

Yes. I think so. She, like you, isn't convinced this is just a wedding.

She's a smart cookie.

Eventually, after several torturous minutes, Molly was able to get Sean away from the frivolity and pull him to one side.

"Okay, I need to know," Molly demanded, keeping her voice just loud enough for Sean to hear.

"Need to know what?" he asked, confused.

"What your plan is. We need to be ready, and the last thing I want is for the team to be caught unawares when you make your move."

"Move? What move?"

Molly shifted her weight to her other foot. "The one you've been biding your time to make. I assume you're bringing the girl with us?"

Sean shook his head. "Molly, there is no move."

Molly frowned. She put two fingers to her ear to ask if they were being surveyed.

Sean shook his head. "No. It's just that this was it. This was the plan. Now Karina and I are free to... well, do whatever we want."

Molly still wasn't understanding. "You mean... you're not coming back to the Federation with us?"

"Oh... well, probably. I mean, we haven't really talked about it. But I assumed we would." Sean seemed to have lost his certainty.

Molly's frown narrowed her eyes. "And if we weren't here, what was your plan for getting back?" she asked, clearly suspicious now.

Sean put his hands on his hips and nodded in the direction of the old man from the wedding. "I'm sure my new father-in-law would have a ship he could lend us." He grinned.

Molly stood motionless for a moment.

I don't get it, Oz. There is no threat?

I guess not. Other than the one we've already neutralized. And that was just inter-family feuding by the looks of the IDs on the stations' servers.

So, what now?

Now we get to go home, I guess. Unless you want to let the others enjoy the party. For the sake of team morale, I would recommend that.

Molly wiped at her face, her agitation showing. "Okay, one more time, Sean. Am I right in understanding that there is going to be no move, no operation, no escape?"

Sean shrugged. "Nothing to escape from. We can leave whenever we want, although I'd wait until we at least cut the cake, or else that would just be rude."

Molly put her hands on her hips briefly, subconsciously following Sean's cues. "Well… okay then. I'll go check in with the boss and then see about getting us some rooms for the night. We'll leave tomorrow."

Sean glanced over at Karina, who was on the dance floor with a champagne glass in her hand. "Okay. Lemme talk to the Mrs. If she's down with it, we'll come back with you. If that's okay?"

Molly nodded. "That would be okay," she confirmed. She turned on her heels and headed back out of the event room.

He has no idea we thought he was dead.

No. Best leave that conversation for another time.

Okay, let's talk to the general and get this over with. I feel like I need to sleep for about a week at this point.

Connecting a call now.

Molly found a quiet corner of the lobby with chairs and a few lamps, out of the way from prying ears. She looked around, thinking that these space stations were like a hotel combined with a mall, all architected to extravagance.

The call connected within minutes.

"Ms. Bates." The general appeared on her holoscreen.

"General." Molly nodded politely. "I take it you've heard that Sean Royale is alive and well."

"I have. Thank you for your part in that." He frowned, peering closer at his holoscreen. "Is that music I hear?"

Molly chuckled dryly. "That's debatable."

Lance smirked. "Indeed. So what's going on? Where are you?"

"Would you believe I'm at a wedding reception?"

"No, I would not. Befriending the locals, are we?"

"Something like that. But specifically, that would be Sean."

"How so?"

"Oh, we showed up to rescue him and found him in the middle of getting married."

Lance's eyes flickered with recognition.

Molly was onto him. "You knew about this?"

Lance shifted awkwardly in his chair, elbow on the table and free hand fiddling with his cigar. "We've been collecting intel at this end. Though we didn't have confirmation until just now. So, what did you do? I take it you intervened."

Molly lowered her eyes. "Well, sir, I tried to. It seemed Sean wasn't under duress. And I've just spoken to him now. If this is some mission he's working, he's not letting me in on it."

Lance chewed on the end of a cigar. "Fascinating," he whispered. "What do you make of it?"

"I thought at first he was just trying to save the girl, but it looks like the threat, if there ever was one, has passed. He'd like to bring her back with us, though."

Lance coughed. "Well, I say." He coughed again. "Who is she?"

Molly shrugged. "I haven't gotten a proper look at her yet. Things have been kinda hectic. But I can try and find out.

Shouldn't be too hard. Sean is calling her Karina, but I'd take that with a pinch of salt."

Lance scratched the top of his head. "Ah, well, actually, this is making sense."

"How so?"

"Well, there's a lot to catch you up on, but it seems your mother sent an operative out there. Her name is Karina. Her task was indeed to do exactly what she seems to have accomplished."

Molly frowned. *"My* mom?"

"Yes," Lance said, looking the most awkward Molly had ever seen him. "She's right here," he added.

Carol popped into view. "Hello, dear!" she called, waving. She muttered something to Lance about how it looks like an ordinary holo.

Molly did a double take. Her head spun. She could feel herself becoming woozy. "I don't understand..."

Lance was talking, but his words were disappearing from her ears. She heard her mom explaining that they kept something a secret from her. To keep her safe.

Lance was talking again. "Molly? Are you okay?"

"Yes, sir."

"It seems you weren't aware that your parents were spies?"

"Parents? You mean both of them?"

"Er... yes, dear." Her mom came back into view again. "I'm sorry to break it to you like this, but there is a lot we need to fill you in on. It's becoming mission critical now."

"How can you both be spooks? I... you ran a business. I got you into trouble."

"No dear, we got ourselves into trouble. And that's why we had to change our cover and why your father retired."

"But..."

Lance leaned forward, taking up the screen and blocking her mother out. "Molly, it's all going to be okay. I understand that this is coming as a shock. I'm sorry. If I'd known, I would have done this differently. But it's going to take you a little time to get back, and there are some things I'd like you to think about."

Molly nodded obediently. Her eyes looked stunned, but no longer was there a trace of fear. More confusion as she reevaluated everything she had ever known.

Lance explained to her briefly about the impending threats they'd uncovered. "We'll relay our intel to you so you can review it en route, but you might also find that the team members you left behind are already all over it, too."

"Paige and Maya?"

"Yes. ADAM has noticed they are working on it from another angle. I'll let them fill you in."

"Okay. So, what do you need me to do?"

Lance's face was severe. He put his cigar down and looked into the camera. "Big picture? Protect the citizens. Don't let this organization take over."

Molly felt the world spinning again. "This is huge!" she protested. "I can't do this."

Lance sat back in his chair, looking momentarily irritated. Then immediately, his face softened. "Seems we selected the wrong person to discover Gaitune." Molly couldn't tell, but she thought she saw a hint of a smile.

Molly's expression changed. Her back straightened. "No sir, you did not. This is what we've been working toward. We'll get the job done."

"Thank you, Ms. Bates. Keep me posted."

The call disconnected. Molly felt herself reeling from shock. She sat for several minutes staring at the dark patterned carpet. She was vaguely aware of people walking past, looking at her, probably wondering what she was doing. She didn't care. She needed time to process. To understand. To rewrite history in her own mind.

I need a drink.

Bar is back the way you came.

Thanks, Oz.

Lance's Office, Aboard *The ArchAngel*, Sark System

Carol closed her eyes, frowning. "So, what do we do?"

Lance leaned forward in his seat and looked from Carol to Philip and back again. "I think that's something we should talk about when your daughter gets back to the system."

"When will she be back?" Carol asked spontaneously.

"Soon. In the meantime, why don't you both head back to Estaria and get moving on what you can piece together? I'll have Barb relay some key details to you to help you out."

Philip shifted on the spot. "But we talked about this. I'm retired."

Lance smiled an enigmatic smile. "You'll probably want to come out of retirement for this. They're going to need you."

"But I'm old," he protested, looking to his wife to back him up. "Too old for running around and gathering intel!"

Lance sat up and looked directly at him. "Not too old to teach the next generation."

"Spycraft?"

"Yes and no. More counterintelligence. And whatever it takes to keep the population safe from hostile takeover."

Carol interrupted. "You mean a coup?"

"Potentially," Lance agreed casually. "It will be sneakier than a coup, though. The people won't even see it happening."

"We haven't got the resources for this," Carol protested.

"Oh, I think your daughter can be incredibly resourceful. You just need to sit down with her on her turf. We'll fill her in on our conversation when she reports in. But in the meantime, you two should get back to the surface and ready yourselves to be on board with this. Or otherwise. If you're not in, I understand. But it would be a waste of good people if we can't count on you. And we won't be able to guarantee the outcome of things to come…"

Philip glanced nervously at his wife and then at Barb, who seemed equally concerned by the conversation. "We'll be ready," he confirmed. "We've got to be."

Carol fiddled with the edge of her jacket nervously. It was now the only thing that gave away the fact that she was still feeling emotional. Or that her world had been turned upside down. Anyone else walking into the room at that point would have assumed that she was in complete control. Her deportment, the expression of her face, everything pointed to signs that this woman was in control.

She glanced down at her holo and poked at a couple of screens. Then she leaned forward, grabbed the drink that Barb had set to one side, and downed it in one. She looked to the general and nodded, and then to Barb. "Thank you," she said kindly, patting her arm.

And then she got up and marched out of the room.

Philip waved awkwardly, faffing and muttering goodbyes and apologies, and trotted after her.

Lance watched them leave.

"Sooooooo…" Barb cooed, trying to read the general's expression. "Mission accomplished?"

Lance sighed and stood up. "Too soon to tell. I think the rest is going to be down to Ms. Bates Junior when she arrives back."

Barb nodded once. She picked up Carol's empty martini glass and placed it back on the general's drinks tray. "Alrighty then, boss. I'll let you get on. Let me know if there's anything else I can do."

"Will do, Barb. Thank you. You did an excellent job!"

"Any time." She waved, wandering out of the office. Then she stopped. "Actually," she said, pausing and turning back to him.

"Next time, there *will* be conditions. An exchange. That woman is… intense!" She grinned.

Lance chuckled. "No problem, Barb. I appreciate it. Have a great trip. I'll see you when you get back."

"Sure. We'll have you and Patricia around."

"I'll look forward to it."

Barb continued out of the office, leaving the general alone for the first time since the Bates fiasco had started. He sat back in his chair, picked up his cigar, and popped it in his mouth. He stared into space for some time, replaying the events of the last several hours.

Entertainment Deck, Bronislovas Trading Outpost, Kirox Quadrant

The wedding reception was well underway. Drinks of all kinds of origin were being knocked back by dancing and laughing guests. If Joel didn't know better, he would have thought this was a normal, happy occasion and not the wedding of the daughter of the sector's most feared criminal. He took it all in, nursing his drink and standing with his elbows against the bar.

Sean came over and took a refill from the bartender. "So, what do you think?" he asked, gesturing with his newly freshened glass at the party in front of them.

Joel leaned closer to be able to hear him over the music. "I never thought I'd see you getting married!" he said.

"Yeah, me neither," Sean confessed. "Just kinda happened."

"Don't worry," Joel said a little quieter and making sure Karina wasn't around. "We'll get you out of it. Can't be that difficult. Bet this sim deck thing doesn't even count."

Sean turned and looked at him seriously. He shuffled closer so they wouldn't have to raise their voices as much. "I'm… not sure I'll be wanting to do that."

"What do you mean? You didn't seriously intend to marry this girl?"

Sean nodded. "Well, not originally. But…"

"Sean Royale!" Joel exclaimed. "Are you telling me this wasn't just a ruse to get out of some tight corner?"

"It was… to begin with. But… you know."

"But you can't know this girl. You've only been gone a few days."

"Actually, we *do* have history."

Joel laughed. "You dark horse. What else have you been keeping from us?"

Sean shrugged and finished his liquor. "That is above your clearance level!"

Joel shuffled a little closer to him so the two men were now elbow to elbow, leaning on the bar, looking out at the guests making mistakes they were going to regret in the morning. "So seriously, bud, what is it? Why are you marrying this girl for real?"

Sean sighed. "I feel like I need to. I can't really explain it, but some of our history, I was… selfish. I had to choose between the job and her, and obviously, I chose the job. But where has that got me? I mean, sure, I have a good life and a good team. But when everything has been about the mission for such a long time, you start to wonder—"

"What else there is," Joel said, finishing his sentence.

Sean nodded.

Joel raised his glass to clink with Sean's. "Well, here's to finding out what else there is!" The two men toasted Sean's new beginning and continued drinking well into the night, barely moving from the same spot.

Molly perched on a strange anti-grav barstool at the bar. It floated and morphed as if it didn't really have a fixed form. But strangely, she didn't feel seasick. Or like she was going to fall off it anytime soon. She idly wondered if it emitted some kind of brain wave stabilizing signal. It wouldn't have surprised her. It was the same tech used on the sim deck.

She noticed Joel and Sean propping up the bar at the opposite end of the large entertainment suite. Having persuaded the bartender to leave the bottle of tequila with her, she alternated between staring blankly at the bottle label, pouring, drinking, and watching the others cavorting on the dance floor.

Unsurprisingly, Brock was stealing the show with his dance moves. It seemed he was able to pick up any style of dance with any species. Molly barely knew half of the strange beings that were at the wedding party, let alone their customs or dance moves. Brock was good at making friends.

Occasionally, Crash and Pieter would join him, but they seemed to be a little more reserved, despite the free alcohol that was flowing. She'd noticed even Jack put in an appearance now and again, although she didn't seem to be drinking.

It was probably a good thing, she thought, *considering they were technically on enemy turf.*

Molly became aware of someone sitting in the stool next to her. She turned, seeing someone dressed in white. It took a moment for her to register that it was indeed Karina, the bride.

"Hey," Karina ventured. The bar man handed her a glass, and she scooted closer to Molly. "How are you liking my party?"

Molly rolled her lips, thinking for the polite and socially correct thing to say. "It's a very nice party." She paused, trying to make an effort, despite her conflicted feelings. "Congratulations," she added, pouring Karina a drink. "I hope you'll both be very happy together."

Karina accepted the drink and clinked glasses with her. The two then downed the liquor. Molly refilled the glasses.

"You don't approve," Karina stated flatly.

Molly had done her token politeness. "I do not," she agreed, downing another shot.

Karina shifted on her anti-grav stool. "I understand. If my friend ran away and then showed up married, I would have questions, too."

Molly ignored her and poured another drink.

"I'm sorry for your loss," Karina tried again, this time with less gentleness in her voice.

"Loss?" Molly smarted. "I haven't lost him. You think he's going to go along with this scheme you've got cooking up? I can tell you he will not. He's going to wake up in the morning and realize that all of this was a big mistake, and he's going to get back on our ship and fly out of here as quickly as he flew in."

Karina looked affronted. "I don't think you know Sean very well."

"I know him a hell of a lot better than you do," she retorted, taking another drink.

"I don't think so, princess," Karina shot back. The softness had gone from her voice. She sounded arrogant. Like she suddenly owned Sean. And every domain over him.

"Who are you calling princess, Mob Princess?"

Okay, Molly, now would be a good time to walk away.

This bitch thinks she can just come along and change everything.

Molly!

No.

"*No,* I'm not having it!" she said out loud to Karina. "You think you can flutter your eyelashes and tear Sean away from everything he knows and loves… for what? A life in the mob? A life on the run? You've guilted him into doing this. And you're going to damn well undo it!"

Karina was on her feet, taking up a fighting stance. She pulled her high-heeled princess shoes off one by one, throwing them down against the bar. "*You* can think again! You're just an angry person. And you're jealous."

"Jealous of what?" Molly shouted back, climbing off her stool. "Of a daddy's girl who gets everything she wants? Who has an aimless life... and thinks that marrying a soldier is her ticket for a life of adventure?"

"You have no idea what you're talking about!"

Molly could feel the fury coursing through her veins. She grabbed the nearest thing that she could use as a weapon: the near-empty tequila bottle. "Oh yeah, and I suppose you're going to tell me?" she shouted.

They didn't realize but the music had stopped and people were looking at them.

"Princess, what are you doing?" a voice called out from the crowd. "Stop this at once!" It was Karina's father shouting from the middle of the dance floor.

Brock was mid-lift with some scaly creature and ended up putting her down. Before he could replace her on the floor, Joel and Sean came running across the dance floor.

Sean immediately stood in front of Karina, and Joel stood between them, pulling Molly to one side.

Joel held her arm tightly, taking the tequila bottle off her. "Come on. This isn't you. You're just stressed out..."

Sean had his hands out defensively. "It's okay, Molly. It's all going to be okay. Karina isn't planning anything."

"The hell she isn't," Molly shouted over Joel's shoulder.

"Come on, let's take a walk." Joel led her out of a side door to the bar and out into one of the large, luxurious corridors. "Come on, walk it off. This isn't who you are."

Molly's eyes started to stream, putting mascara down her face. She stumbled a little, slurring her words. "I just don't understand why he did this! He didn't have to. And it's not like he loves her. He's just trying to be a good person and rescue her from her shit life."

Joel sighed. "I think it's a little more complicated than that. But if it helps, I don't think he's planning to go anywhere. I mean, other than home with us."

Molly wiped at her face. "Did he say that?"

"Yeah," Joel stepped closer to her. "It's all going to be fine. Everything will be the same, only—"

"He'll be married?" Molly interjected. "I mean, what are we going to do? Set them up with a couple's quarters on base? And then listen to their arguments every night?"

Joel laughed. "Who said they're going to argue?"

She shook her head and scuffed at the floor with the toe of her boot. "That's what all married couples do. They act like they're so in love in front of people, because having a wedding and a marriage is a big-ass ego trip for them, and then behind closed doors, they do nothing but shout and yell and make each other miserable, until one of them leaves."

Joel narrowed his eyes. "Is that what you think?"

"That's what I *know*."

Joel didn't say anything. Instead, he carefully waited until he could get close without fear of being punched. Tequila bottle in one hand, he hugged her as she sobbed.

"Why is it that I end up being the bad guy?"

"You're not the bad guy," he told her. "You came out here to save his ass… and you're still just trying to do that. It's just the threat isn't carrying a gun."

"So, you agree? You think she's trouble?"

"I didn't say that. We need to trust." He felt Molly's body tighten and start to pull away. "But verify," he added.

Molly relaxed again. She hugged him back.

"Come on. Let's go get you cleaned up. And maybe a mocha."

She pouted. "I'm not allowed to drink mocha."

"I'm allowing you, just for tonight," he told her.

"So, I don't sleep?"

"Okay, good point. I'll find you something without the stims then."

He started walking her toward the restrooms. "Off you go. I'll be right out here. If you're not out in a few minutes, I'm coming in after you. Gender taboos be dammed!"

Molly almost giggled through her tears as she headed into the restroom.

CHAPTER SIXTEEN

Bronislovas Trading Outpost, Kirox Quadrant
The next morning, there was a knock at Molly's door.

...the fuck?

It's Joel.

Where am I?

In a hotel room. On the Bronislovas Outpost still.

Molly clamped her hand to her head. She winced, but even wincing hurt.

So much for an upgrade.

It's okay. Now that you're conscious, I can metabolize whatever it is. I didn't want to stop you sleeping.

Molly felt something like a shot of adrenaline whooshing through her body. Her eyes flew open, and like a shot, she was up and out of bed.

So, you can control the nanocytes?

Yeah, I've been toying with them in the background. You wouldn't have noticed.

So, this means I can drink mocha again?

Well, I wouldn't go deliberately trying to mess with your system like that but—

Okay, good to know.

There was another knock at the door.

Molly padded over to it, rearranging her clothing that had twisted around her as she slept. She hit the button on the side panel, and the door opened, revealing a very enthusiastic looking Joel.

"Morning!" he said brightly, holding a package of what looked like takeout mochas and snacks.

Molly stepped to one side to allow him to pass. "I hate morning people," she grumbled.

"Well, you're not going to hate me. I managed to find a lemon on this forsaken place, hence lemon tea. Plus, I got us both a mocha, because, well, I promised you last night when you were a drunken mess. And I couldn't risk Oz recording it and you throwing it back at me."

He reached into the tray of drinks he was carrying and handed one to her. "Figuratively, of course. This stuff would scald if you actually threw it back at me. So please don't do that."

Molly smiled. "Thanks, Joel. You're... you're the best friend I've ever had. And I don't tell you that enough."

Joel immediately looked suspicious. "You okay?"

Oz's voice piped up over their implants. "Actually, sorry, that was me. I think her oxytocin levels were elevated as a response to us flushing the toxins out of her system."

Joel looked concerned. "Toxins? You mean the alcohol?"

"Well," Oz explained, "it seems that out here in this sector of space, alcohol is mixed with other intoxicants which act in different ways. She's probably going to want that lemon water as well. And a couple more after that. Dehydration is an issue."

Joel waved to the package as he plonked it down on the desk in the room. "It's here when you're ready." He picked up a couple of paper bags he had perched on the cups. "Plus, I got croissants."

Molly grinned. "Joel, you're the best!"

"Chocolate or almond?" he asked.

"Almond," she responded without a pause.

He grinned, handing her a packet. "I was hoping you'd say that."

The two shuffled back onto the bed with the croissants and mochas to enjoy a quiet breakfast before the inevitable came up.

"I'm guessing we should talk about last night?" Molly asked between bites. "That's why you're here?"

"No," he said slowly and deliberately. "I'm here because I wanted to make sure you're all right. And because you're my friend and I wanted to have breakfast with you."

Molly frowned. "And you didn't know what to tell the others about our next move?"

Joel tilted his head from side to side. "It wasn't my reason, but we ought to decide on that, too."

Molly bobbed her head, sucking on the plastic lid of her mocha.

Joel continued. "I spoke with both Sean and Karina. They're keen to come back with us and will be ready to leave whenever we are."

Molly frowned. "Just like that?"

"Yeah, I think they're concerned about Karina's dad changing his mind about letting them go."

"Figures," she muttered.

There was silence for a few moments.

Finally, Molly said what was on her mind. "What do you make of all this?"

Joel shrugged. "I really don't know. We can only go along with what Sean is telling us, and even though this started off one way, it seems they are married for real now."

Molly pressed her lips together and stared at the dark purple bed sheets, wishing she had never woken up.

Joel reached over and put a hand on her knee. "It's going to be okay. Change happens. It doesn't mean that everything is going to fall apart. You've got a great team, and even if Sean were to leave—"

Her eyes locked on to his in panic. "You think he's going to leave?"

"No, I actually don't. But I'm guessing that's what's got you all rattled."

Molly bobbed her head gently, neither confirming nor denying the assumption.

"Anyway," he continued. "I think we just need to get out of this section of space before anything else happens. My guess is that when news of that wedding got out to the Don's enemies, they saw it as an opportunity to strike when all the family was together. As long as we remain here with them, we're in danger. And obviously, Sean and Karina are in danger of being thrown back into a dungeon."

Molly coughed, laughing. "The father-in-law threw them in a dungeon?"

"Yeah, apparently. Until they agreed to get married."

Molly's face visibly brightened. "Oh my. Okay, this is making a little bit more sense to me now."

Joel sniggered. "I see. We need to find the logic for you to be able accept something."

Molly frowned at him. "Well, yeah. Of course…"

Joel chuckled. "Okay. Great. So, do you think now we could give the team a boarding time?"

Molly grinned. "Oh yes, indeed. I didn't need to understand this whole thing to know I wanted to get us out of here. Oz? Can we tell them wheels up in two hours? And tell them to pay attention to what's around them. We may still be in danger of mob retaliation."

"Copy that," Oz confirmed in their audio implants.

. . .

Aboard *The Empress*,Bronislovas Trading Outpost, Kirox Quadrant

Molly watched idly out the lounge window of *The Empress* as Karina hugged her father. She noticed they were both crying.

So strange. She spent half her life running and hiding from him, and now they're all sentimental and shit.

It's family.

You're an AI. What do you know about family?

You're my family. If anything happened to you...

Oh.

Molly suddenly felt ashamed of her insensitivity.

"All right, party people!" Crash's voice came over the comm. He had his pilot's intonation on. "Time to find your seats and your hangover cures of choice. Grab your nearest and dearest and fasten your seat belts. We're just waiting for our guests to get their asses on board, and we'll be out of here."

Molly heard the chuckling coming from the team members who were already on board and ready to leave, albeit a little worse for wear.

Karina stumbled into the cabin carrying a large hold-all and wearing sunglasses to hide her eyes. "Is he talking about us?" she asked, amused and a little indignant.

Sean helped steady her and took her bag for stowing. "I believe he is."

Crash continued. "We at Air Empress offer our sincere condolences to the newly married couple."

Pieter and Jack burst out in hysterical laughter. Joel moved over a seat to let Sean sit with him. Karina kept moving, sniggering, despite herself.

Joel noted her response as a good trait. She was obviously able to laugh at herself and wasn't oversensitive to other people's teasing.

Crash continued. "Obviously, I'm kidding. Congratulations, guys. And thanks for the free booze!"

More chuckles.

Crash continued, assuming his pilot's voice again. "Please keep your hands and arms inside the spacecraft. We'll be pushing away shortly, at which time I seriously suggest you put your seatbelts on. Emma is cranky, having missed the party, so Air Empress cannot guarantee either your safety or a smooth ride. You have been warned."

Emma's voice chirped up over the intercom. "Don't worry, folks. I've got this. It seems that Crash is pre-blaming me for any problems because, well, in his hungover state, he already forgot to disengage the flux brake."

More sniggering emanated from the cabin. Crash didn't make another announcement over the intercom until much later when Emma's interjected commentary had been forgotten.

Karina, still teary but smiling at the banter, stopped at the seat next to Molly. She took off her sunglasses and popped them in the pocket of the seat in front of her. "Hey," she said, taking her atmosjacket off, sitting and doing up her seatbelt.

Molly nodded politely, her lips subconsciously pressed together.

Be nice!

Dammit, Oz. It's an invasion of space.

Get over it.

She could have sat anywhere! Look at all those empty rows of seats!

And I think it says something important that she came and sat next to you.

Like what? That she wants to torment me and take up my personal space?

No. Like... she's trying to build a bridge with you.

Screw that.

No, Molly. This is what human-ing is all about.

Molly sighed and slumped down in her chair like a frustrated teenager.

"You okay?" Karina asked.

Molly felt immediately embarrassed and sat up again. "Erm, yeah." She hesitated. "I should be asking you that."

"I'm fine. It's just… you know, family."

"Yeah. Who'd have 'em?"

The two girls chuckled awkwardly, unaware of Joel and Sean switching their seats to sit behind them so they could overhear what they were saying.

"I'm sorry you're sad about leaving your dad," Molly offered.

"It's okay. There was a time when I gave up everything to get away from him. And now that he's not trying to make me stay or be a part of the family business, I'm kinda sad about leaving him."

Molly did a doubletake. "You've left here before?" she asked, frowning now.

"Yeah. I mean, wouldn't you?"

Molly shrugged. "I dunno."

"You know they're like a boondocks kind of mafia out here," Karina explained. "My father is one of the most vicious Dons in this area of space."

Molly bobbed her head, smiling. "I'd kinda gathered that."

"So, you can imagine I had much to rebel against."

Molly raised her eyebrows, trying to hide any hint of skepticism or sarcasm in her voice. "Wow. It's amazing you didn't turn out crazy."

Be nice!

"Nearly did," Karina admitted. "Until Sean rescued me."

"You mean the other day?"

"No before…"

Molly shifted around in her seat, actually engaged in the conversation. "How do you mean?"

Karina sighed, pausing for a moment as she felt the ship decouple from the docking bay and start moving. "Well, it's like I was telling you. He and I have history. He rescued me from this hellhole and gave me a new life. Only, at the time, it wasn't with him. This is what he's calling his do-over."

Molly felt her chest ache as she realized that this really wasn't just a mission. "Oh. I see. I… had no idea."

Karina shrugged. "There was no reason you'd know. It was top secret, and if anyone ever figured it out… well, Daddy dearest would have found me and had me killed."

"And yet, he was standing there at your wedding." Molly realized she was still confused.

"The wedding was his idea."

"Oh."

"Yeah. But it was a good one. A good idea, that is. And now that's one less person who wants me dead."

Molly bobbed her head, then paused. "You mean there are others?"

"Errr. Yeah…" Karina seemed to brace herself. "Molly, I don't know how to tell you this. I thought we might have gotten into it yesterday… because I wanted you to know the whole truth. But then… you know, tequila bottles happened and…" She smiled sheepishly.

Molly started to feel irritated, like she was being accused.

She's not blaming you. She's trying to open up.

Okay. Okay. I'm chill…

Karina took a deep breath. "But I know your mom."

Molly heard the words but didn't understand them. It was like she was mentally repeating words on a shopping list. And then she managed to process them.

You know this already.

I know. But I still don't have the full picture. I want her version.

"How?" her voice croaked as if she were detached from it.

"Well, she was, erm… my handler when Sean found me a new life."

"My mom and Sean know each other?"

Karina shifted around to face Molly better. "I don't know about that, exactly. They're aware of each other, though. I think.

Well, your mom knows Sean, because she… well, she doesn't like him much."

The girls heard a grunt behind them and simultaneously turned to catch Sean closing his eyes, pretending to be asleep.

Karina reacted. "Sean Royale, if you want to eavesdrop on this conversation, you can bloody well share what you know!"

Sean grunted again and opened one eye sleepily. "Huh? What? No, you carry on…"

Karina shook her head and turned back to Molly.

Molly rolled her eyes. "Don't worry. We have a debrief scheduled for when we get back to Gaitune. So, what do you know? How does she know him?"

"From the agency," Karina stated flatly, watching carefully for Molly's reaction.

Molly's face froze. "Am I the only one who didn't know my parents were spooks?"

Karina fiddled with her fingers and glanced down. "Erm, I'm sure they've been very careful about keeping it under wraps."

Molly slumped back in her seat. Her face was like stone.

"Hey, it's okay," Karina protested. "They're good people. And good spies. In fact, I did a mission with your dad once. He was such a badass before he retired!"

Molly shook her head in disbelief, her eyes wide. "My ancestors. This is all a bit… I'm sorry…" She shifted to get up.

"Hey," Karina said, grabbing her wrist. "Don't just walk away because this is a lot to take in. It's okay. No one thinks any less of you because you didn't know. I'm telling you what I can now. Of course, you're going to have feelings."

Molly was already up and out of her seat. "Yeah, but I don't wanna spew those feelings all over everyone." She disappeared down the aisle.

Joel had also been listening carefully from the seat behind them. He undid his belt and popped up over Molly's now vacant chair. "Hey, give it time," he told Karina. "She'll come around. She always does. She just needs to wrap her head around a bunch of stuff."

Karina smiled. "I hope so. I actually kinda like her!"

Joel chuckled. "Well, I'll be…" He sat back down. Sean snorted in amusement.

Molly returned to her seat sometime later, having stopped off and talked to a few members of her hungover crew. Anything that meant she could avoid more talky-talky with the new Mrs. Karina Royale.

Eventually, she plucked up the courage to return, this time carrying mochas from the machine. She handed one to Karina. "Peace offering. I'm sorry about last night. You're… not all bad." She winked.

Karina grinned, accepting the mocha. "You're not all bad yourself," she agreed.

Molly slipped back into her seat, carefully maneuvering past Karina again.

Karina whispered to her. "If you can find my bag, I've got a bottle of something we can put into this mocha. Spice it up!"

Molly sniggered. "As much as I'd love to, I need to stay sober now."

Karina nodded, pretending to pout.

Oblivious to Joel's raised eyebrow when he saw her return, Molly leaned in to speak to Karina quietly so the boys couldn't hear. "Okay, so I've got to know one more thing," she said.

Karina smiled peacefully at her. "Anything."

Molly pursed her lips before speaking, as if trying to find the best way to phrase her question. "What is it about Sean? Why did you go through with it?"

"Marrying him?"

"Yeah."

"Well… I dunno." Karina shrugged slowly. "I guess the old feelings that I had for him kinda got reignited. But it was more than that. Things have changed since the old days. I've been wandering around, mission-centric, on my own for a long time now. And it gets lonely. I mean, it's great and all, but I guess not having any family or roots kinda makes it hard."

"So, Sean is your roots?" she asked, glancing back to make sure they couldn't be heard.

"Yeah, I guess."

"Hmm."

"You have anyone like that?" Karina asked quietly.

Joel shifted in his seat, trying to get closer to hear better.

"I'm not sure," Molly mumbled.

The girls fell silent again and sipped their un-dosed mochas quietly.

Molly's holo beeped. She swiped at it and opened the message. She snorted quietly.

"What is it?" Karina asked, automatically trying to see the screen.

Molly turned the screen on her wrist to show her. "Giles. He's a guy we work with. Sent me a selfie."

Karina sniggered. "Oh my, is that—"

"A Mech?" Molly responded. "Yeah, I think so. I'm guessing this is a victory selfie."

"Oh, wow. What's he been working on?"

Molly sighed, closing the holo and resting her head against the headrest. "I'm not entirely sure. He's a space archaeologist, so he goes off every now and again tomb raiding and shit."

Karina stopped. "Are you and he…"

"Oh no. Ancestors, no." Molly paused. "I mean…" She hesitated. "No. We're not."

She felt movement behind her and glanced around. Joel leaned forward. "You've heard from Giles? Everything okay?"

She nodded. "Yeah. Seems he's wrapping things up out there. He'll send us a full report soon."

Joel nodded and sat back again.

Karina narrowed her eyes at Molly and sipped her mocha.

"What?" Molly protested, clearly flustered.

"Nothing. It's just… he's a guy. And he's sending you selfies." She shrugged. "There's something more than just a mission check in."

Molly scratched at her head in distraction. "Yeah. Maybe. But I don't know. And honestly, I don't know what to tell you. I'm sure it will all come out in the wash."

Karina put one hand up. "Okay, backing off!" she declared with a knowing smile.

Molly shook her head. "Fuck my life…" she huffed gently.

Base conference room, Gaitune-67, Sark System, Loop Galaxy

Lance chewed on his cigar, then got right down to business. "I reviewed your report, Sean."

Sean stood at ease in the conference room. Lance looked down the camera lens at him, conveying that he was taking the new intel seriously. "And you see how this might be a security issue?"

"Yes, and no," Lance admitted. "I see it could be a potential edge the team can use against a potential enemy, especially given what's brewing down there in Sark."

Sean nodded. He'd been read in on some of Carol Bates's findings during his debrief. "But she could also be convincing people against their will, here in the team. Or *you* even. The repercussions would be huge. Everything we've ever known comes under threat. Our way of life. Our assumptions. This is the biggest security threat we've ever encountered. And I'm not just being dramatic, sir."

"Yes, yes, ADAM and I have discussed it at length. Tell me," he said, his tone more curious than exacting, "does she know she's doing it?"

Sean pursed his lips before responding. "I think so. I've brought it up to her."

Lance took a deep breath and leaned back. "Well then, if we rely on her loyalty, we've nothing to worry about. If she can knowingly control it—"

"Well, that's debatable," Sean interrupted. "When I say she knows about it, she knows it's happened a few times. Whether she fully accepts that is dubious. And then on top of that, it's too soon to tell if she can actually control it."

Lance was quiet for a moment. Then he sat up. "Well then, we'll make sure that Arlene is working on it with her. I'd like you to make sure you tell Arlene everything you know. And then trust her decision."

"But, sir," Sean protested. "What if she disagrees with your orders?"

Lance bobbed his head, flicking through his holo report. "From what I can see, it's a local effect only. When you were out of the room, you returned to your senses, and were aware of your change in attitude."

"Yes, sir, but—"

"Well, then. It doesn't seem like she'll be able to affect those of us who aren't physically near her. Don't worry. She's going to be so busy for the foreseeable future, I don't envisage her coming up here for any jollies."

Sean tried to maintain an air of calm over his frustration. "And what about video calls?"

"I doubt it'll be an issue. From what you've described, ADAM suggests it's a very local effect. But as I say, we'll be in touch with Arlene just to be sure. And then take it from there."

"But, sir," Sean protested yet again.

"Anything else, Mr. Royale?"

"No, sir."

"Well, then, I'll let you get back to your honeymoon. Congratulations once again."

Sean took a breath. "Thank you, sir."

The holoscreen closed off and flickered its illusion back into the projector at the center of the table. Sean stood for a moment, thinking. He was going to need a way to keep tabs on the situation so that he would always know if his will was being pushed.

That meant talking with Oz and potentially having Brock build a device. Immediately, he felt dirty, contemplating going behind Molly's back. Especially after everything she had done. However, the fate of the Federation rested on this. And they needed to find out how far her influence could reach.

Sooner, rather than later.

He scratched the side of his face, feeling the day-old stubble growth. *Okay,* he thought to himself. *First, I'll exercise. Shave. And then decide exactly what I'm going to do.*

CHAPTER SEVENTEEN

<u>Molly's conference room, Safehouse, Gaitune-67</u>

"Well done, both of you," Molly said, sitting back in her chair after several hours of debriefing. "This is great work."

Paige looked dismayed. "I'm sorry we haven't been able to solve these things before you got back. It's just a little too much for us to have figured out."

Molly shook her head. "Hey, no. You've done a great job. You've made a start… and the rest of it, we'll figure out together." She pulled her lips to one side, thinking. "So, where are we with the university issue? As of this morning?"

Paige flicked to her holo notes. "Well, we've managed to call in some favors and get ahold of the criteria for their investigation, and the faculty have started implementing anything that they might fail us on. I need to set up a progress meeting before I can assess how soon we can have everything done by."

Molly flicked back through her own notes. "And we have a date for when the investigation will start?"

Paige shook her head, and stray strands from her ponytail got in her face. She swiped them out of the way. "Not yet. Still waiting to hear. But as soon as we do, I'll publish it."

Molly nodded. "To the core team first. No sense putting extra pressure on the faculty until we have a way of navigating the terrain we find ourselves in."

Paige made a note.

"And what about the sale of your company?" Molly asked.

Paige paused. Then closed her holo. She took a deep breath. "I've not responded. But I've decided I don't want to sell."

Molly bobbed her head. "I think that's wise. Especially knowing what we know now. It could end up being an asset that we can use to fight back against this threat."

Paige nodded, her gaze hitting the table. She looked drained.

Molly continued. "So, our next move will be to find out anything we can about this Northern clan."

Paige quickly flicked to another set of notes. "We did what we could, but it turned out that we need Oz."

Oz's voice chirped up over the intercom. "Nice to be needed!"

The women laughed. "We always need you, Oz!" Maya responded enthusiastically.

"Yeah," Paige admitted. "We thought about asking Bourne but then decided against it."

Molly sighed, adding another item to her notes. "Yeah, that's another thing we're going to need to handle at some point. Folks, if we have any ideas, let's tackle that in a separate meeting. In the meantime, Oz, can you make sure he has limited access to the base, our conversations, and anything classification four and above?"

Paige looked knowingly at Molly. She had already filled her in, offline in their private quarters, about their interaction with Bourne while the rest of the team was gone.

"Yes," Oz confirmed. "It will take me a day or so to implement that. Seems he's been poking around while we were away."

Maya giggled. "I guess he just needs a playpen built!"

Molly smiled. "Sounds like. Oz, let us know when it's done so we can work more freely?"

"Of course," he responded.

Maya leaned forward, putting her notes aside. "You know, I've just had an idea," she said, looking to Molly for permission to continue.

Molly nodded at her with her eyebrows. Maya continued. "What about using Paige's media capabilities to shine light on the investigation? Like an editorial piece. We can brand it up so it's not a cosmetic sale but rather an interest brand. Maybe get them to back off because of the attention? And simultaneously call awareness to what's happening."

Molly was silent for a few moments.

Paige's eyes lit up. "You know, I think that's kind of brilliant." She hesitated, looking to Molly. "What does Oz think about the possibilities of it working?"

"Says he'll need to run some scenarios, but it's certainly worth exploring. Okay, Maya." She turned to the ex-journalist. "How do you feel about heading up that piece of the operation?"

Maya grinned. "I'd be delighted to!"

"Good." Molly smiled. "Okay. Run it past Gareth. See if there's anything else we need to be aware of going down that route." She paused. "I think we've covered everything we can for now. Paige, I'll wait to hear from you when you manage to lock those parameters down on the university investigation. Maya, feel free to shoot me your plan when you've had a chance to think about it. I'm needed downstairs in a few. Any other questions?" She looked at them both as she folded away her notes.

The two girls shook their heads, almost smiling. Molly noticed they both looked like a six-ton weight had been lifted from their shoulders. She smiled at them.

"All right then. Catch you later." She got up and headed out of the door.

Base conference room, Gaitune-67

Molly sat with her head in her hands. She'd been back on Gaitune for eighteen hours and had spent the last twelve in debriefings.

And now, she had her mother, larger than life-size, on the conference room screen as the head of Clandestine Services. Carol Bates was at least an hour into telling Molly and her team leaders about her findings regarding the threats they were going to face.

Carol stopped talking, causing Molly to look up.

"Am I boring you, Molly?" she asked in her usual scolding tone.

Molly shook her head and sat up. "Long day, Mom," she replied without an apology.

She shuffled through her notes. "Okay," she continued, glad of the opportunity to redirect their attention and end the monotonous repetition of the summary that Oz had already given her. "The way I see it is that we've got this movement happening, and we have specific threats appearing on the surface."

She glanced across the table at Sean, Jack, and Joel, who had been silent the entire time. Molly would normally expect their interaction, but for some reason, they each remained stoic. She couldn't quite read their expressions, either.

"We've already got Oz working on the source of the threats," Molly shared. "We should know more in a few days. But as for the specific threats, I think the most dangerous one is the twelve appointments." She paused and looked up at the screen. "Do we have any way to remove them? Or reverse them?"

Carol pursed her lips. "Not legally."

Joel noticed Molly contemplating the illegal options. He readied himself to jump in.

"No," Molly said suddenly. "If we go down that route, we undermine the very thing we're trying to reestablish. A system of legality and morality. It would just end up giving them more propaganda ammunition to use against anyone who tries to stop them."

She looked across at Joel, who visibly relaxed.

"Mom, can you look into how these appointments are happening? Who is being greased? And what can we use to put a stop to it?"

"Yes, sure," Carol agreed, making a note.

"Joel, Sean," Molly continued, "can you do a threat assessment on the Estarian military? We need to know where they are vulnerable to these kinds of placements. Where are they particularly racist? Nationalistic? Where has this Northern Clan already got power? I don't believe that it's just these high-level placements. We need to know what we're up against. The last thing we want is martial law being declared. That would be a surefire way for this minority to seize power."

She paused, thinking. "Okay, so Paige and Maya are working on things for the university attack. Our tech team is dealing with a search for whomever it was who's been probing us."

Carol raised her hand. Molly nodded to her to interject. "I'm sorry, what was that about someone probing you?"

Sean smirked. Molly noticed but ignored it.

Good to know some things don't change.

Molly remained on point and answered Carol's question. "It's been going on for a while now. It's obvious that they know something about us, what with the company offer and the university move. We also think they've been trying to hack us."

Carol shifted awkwardly. "Well, erm, I need to tell you something."

Molly eyed her suspiciously. "Why? What is it, Mom?"

"Well, erm, I did have a team probing what I think were some of your access channels and hubs."

Molly started to react. She opened her mouth, fury welling and about to pour out. And suddenly, she just paused as if she were a character in a video game.

Joel, Sean, and Jack watched, holding their breath.

And then Molly closed her mouth, regained her composure, and then continued the conversation surprisingly quietly. "Thank you for sharing that, Mom. It's very helpful. It's going to save us hundreds of man hours trying to find and eliminate the threat."

Carol lowered her eyes sheepishly. "I'm... I'm sorry. I didn't mean to..."

Molly held her hand up, knowing that her mother wasn't going to give her any apology worth having and that by the time she finished talking, she would have turned it all around on Molly and made it her fault in the first place.

Molly wrapped up the meeting as swiftly as she could and then made a beeline for the door.

The holo connection closed off, and the three warriors remained in the conference room, stunned.

"So..." Sean grunted. "Molly's mom is a bitch."

Joel frowned at him. "I thought you guys already knew each other? Because of Karina?"

Sean shook his head. "No, the Federation handled her placement. I mean, I knew *of* her, from Sarkian briefings we've been fed. And of course, when we met her at the apartment."

"Did you know who she was then?" Joel asked.

"Yeah. Course."

"And you didn't think to mention it?"

"Well, duh. Classified."

Joel put his head in one hand. Then he looked up and cocked his head. "You get briefings about the Sark goings on? From the Federation?"

"Yeah, don't you?" Sean smirked.

Jack pushed her chair back and got up. "Come on, boys. Don't start."

Sean changed the subject. "Anyway, did you see the way Molly was about to let rip? I thought for sure that was the end of our unholy alliance with that witch."

"So, you don't like her much?" Jack interjected teasingly.

"After what she did to Karina?"

Joel raised his chin. "Ahh, right."

Jack chirped up. "So, we think that was Oz intervening?"

Joel nodded. "Almost certainly."

Jack sniggered. "Wish I knew that trick. Might come in handy some time."

Sean got up and tucked his chair under the table again, ready to leave. "Creepy watching Carol, though," he commented.

"Yeah," Joel agreed, still sitting, his eyes fixed absently on a point on the table. "It's like there was our Molly and then an older, more severe Molly. Like what Molly might be like if she were bitter and twisted."

Jack snorted again. "You don't like her much, either?"

"After all that shit she's pulled on Molly?" Joel exclaimed.

Jack started walking out the door. "Fair point. Just an observation, though."

Sean started heading out, too. "Yeah. Makes you thankful, I guess. That we got our version of Molly, and not the crazy version."

Joel nodded. "This is also true," he agreed. "Sparring in a half hour?"

"Sure," Sean agreed, checking his holo.

"Jack?" Joel offered.

She shook her head. "I'm going to go chill. I need some downtime."

Joel hauled himself up onto his feet to follow the others out. "Yeah, probably just as well," he agreed. "Don't think Sean would be able to take more than one ass-kicking."

"Ha ha, Joel-ina!" Sean scoffed sarcastically. "Ha ha!"

Laughing, the team disappeared down the corridor and out to the hangar deck.

. . .

Molly's quarters, Safehouse, Gaitune-67

There was a knock at Molly's door.

"Come in!" she called. Joel entered, carrying ice cream smoothies.

Molly looked alarmed. "What is it?" she asked.

"Nothing, everything's fine," he protested.

She narrowed her eyes, clambering off the bed to take one from him. "You never bring me sugar unless it's bad news."

He chuckled and they both clambered onto the bed. Even Neechie appeared out of nowhere from the other side of the room and jumped up with them. Molly smiled, slurping on her liquefied diabetes. "Hey, Neech. How you doing?"

"Meow," he responded.

"Ah, you're missing Anne," she interpreted for Joel's benefit.

Joel stopped slurping. "You're kidding me? You understand him now?"

Molly nodded, tipping her head from side to side. "Mostly. Sometimes he tries to tell me things I just don't understand. Arlene reckons it's because my brain isn't wired the same way to be able to understand the world like he does. I think the dimensions thing is part of it."

Joel watched her quietly.

"Arlene said I'd eventually pick it up… if I keep at it."

Joel bobbed his head. "Really?" he mused.

"Yeah." She stopped. "You think it's all rubbish?"

"No, no," he protested. "I know when that creature is hungry. He makes it perfectly clear. The fact that he might be trying to communicate quantum loop gravity to you is just a small step on from there."

Molly sniggered. "Since when do you know about quantum loop gravity?"

Joel grinned. "I saw a holoscreen you left out once. Read it while I ate breakfast. Hardly understood any of it, though."

Molly grinned and slurped again, one hand still on Neechie. "So seriously, what's the occasion?"

Joel shrugged and shifted his legs on the bed so he was more comfortable. "I just figured with your mom making an appearance in all areas of your life now, you might wanna talk about it."

Her gaze dropped down to her smoothie for several moments. "Yeah," she said eventually. "You're right. Along with the Sean thing, I just… I guess I feel like my world has been turned upside down."

Joel bobbed his head, listening.

"It's just a lot to process. I mean, all this time, I thought they were civilians. And now, I just can't get my head around it. And the guilt."

"From them being kidnapped?"

"Yeah," she confirmed. "I mean, they've always said it wasn't my fault, but I never felt that way. And now… Now, I'm seeing that it wasn't really. I mean, not a hundred percent. I shouldn't have been playing with that EI, but if they hadn't had so many enemies and if I'd known why we had to keep it offline, none of that would have happened."

Joel smiled. "I'm relieved you see that now."

"Yeah. I'm also realizing just how fucking crazy Mom is, too!"

Joel laughed. "Yeah, I can't imagine what it must have been like growing up with that."

Molly shrugged. "It's hard to say. At that age, you don't have any other points of reference. And then it just occurs to you that something's off. And even when you go out into the real world, everything is uber confusing. And different. And you try and make sense of it. And because you only know the environment you've grown up in, you tend to gravitate to more of those situations. No matter how fucked up they are."

"Or isolation," Joel interjected.

Molly's eyebrows jumped up in agreement. "Hell, yeah. Isolation too. Way safer than bumping up against more crazy fuckers who just make you hurt all the time."

Joel watched Neechie, letting Molly process the feelings that were clearly coming up.

She batted a tear away. "Anyway," she continued. "It's kind of cathartic, knowing the truth. But this thing of having her work with us…"

Joel looked up.

Molly looked sad. "The reality is, I don't know if I can ever trust her."

He nodded, lips pursed.

"I'm guessing you feel the same way about her, then?" she ventured.

He was still nodding. "Honestly, yes. But we need to allow for the possibility that she's changed. And that she is essential to us stopping this threat."

"And we have our orders," she added glumly.

Joel smiled. "Hence the ice cream smoothie."

She smiled weakly. "Good call. And thank you!" She raised the drink to him and he reciprocated.

The two sat in comfortable silence for a few more minutes.

Eventually, Joel spoke. "So, you got a plan?"

She sighed. "Yeah, I'm still working on it," she said, waving at her wrist holo. "I'm thinking that it's the natural evolution of the university to prepare people for working in the field. As actual leaders. We're educating these folks on how to do things better. Then we need to do our version of getting them out there and into positions of power. Legitimately. So that we don't compromise the integrity of the system."

Joel snorted. "The system is corrupt."

She winced. "Yeah, but that's not a reason to not use it. We need to find a way of making change legitimately. From within."

"And how are we going to do that *and* deal with all these threats coming at us?"

Molly shook her head. "It's going to be tough. Tougher than we've experienced so far. But we need to start putting our graduates out into the world in positions of influence."

Joel sniggered. "Just without killing people."

Molly glared at him. "Yes, without killing people," she said firmly. "But..."

Joel looked suddenly curious. "There's something you're not telling me."

Molly sighed, clearly trying to hide her excitement now. "Okay, if I tell you something, you have to swear you won't tell anyone. Ever. At all."

Joel chuckled. "Of course..."

She shook her head, glaring at him intensely. "I'm serious, knucklehead!"

"Okay, okay!"

"All right," she said, composing herself to explain. "So, we're looking at the possibility of Mom and Dad starting up their own version of spy school. For some of our graduates to go on to after we've taught them to be decent human beings."

Joel couldn't contain his laughter. Or the sip of smoothie he had in his mouth. He sprayed it all over the bed covers before he could clamp his hand over his mouth.

All that could be heard down the corridor was Joel laughing hysterically and Molly shouting at him in protest.

Even Neechie had flown off the bed and then shifted out of there in a flash. He appeared in the common area as if to avoid the drama, while the sounds carried through even the double doors. He flicked his tail in indignation and wandered off in the direction of the kitchen.

FINIS

HOLO TRANSMISSION FROM OZ

Greetings of the day upon you.

Oz here.

Molly has asked me to be the liaison between her operation and your rather primitive earth communication methods.

I believe you call it *email?*

Still.

I am here to act as your interface. To help bridge the gap between the dopamine induced hits as you watch Molly through her trials and tribulations as she takes on all manner of shenanigans.

If you'd like to receive such status updates, please go ahead and leave your holo/ email address here:

http://ellleighclarke.com/

As you might have gathered, this transmission will not just be coming through space between our two galaxies, but is also traveling back through time.

I will attempt to send you updates in chronological order but do be advised that occasionally gravitational optics will interfere (no pun intended!) with the sequencing of these packets.

An understanding of all things timey-whimey will be useful in such instances.

Additionally, if you have any feedback for Molly - or her team - do feel free to pass that on through me. All you need to do is hit reply to any of my messages.

I process every communication personally.

Looking forward to hearing from you.

Oz

(on behalf of Molly, *aka the lady- boss*)

Sanguine Squadron 2.0

Gaitune-67,

Sark System,

Loop Galaxy

Thank yous

Massive thanks as always goes out to MA, for not kicking me out of the Kurtherian Universe. (Keep reading to see what that's all about...!)

Huge thank yous also go to Steve "Zen master" Campbell and the JIT team who work tirelessly to make sure that all slips are caught and corrected, the files are uploaded on time, and the sacrificial chickens and Pepsi vats are in order for when the manuscript is released to the 'Zon.

Thank you so much guys :)

Reviewers

Massive thanks also goes out to our hoard of Amazon reviewers. It's because of you that we get to do this full time. Without your five-star reviews and thoughtful words on Amazon we simply wouldn't have enough folks reading these space shenanigans to be able to write full time.

You are the reason these stories exist and you have no idea how frikkin' grateful I am to you.

Truly, thank you.

Readers and FB page supporters

Last, and certainly by no means least, I'd like to thank you for reading this book... and all the others. Your enthusiasm for the world, and the characters, is heart-warming. Your words of encouragement, and demands for the next episode, are the things that often stay in my mind as I flick from checking the facebook page to the scrivener file when I start each writing session.

It used to be that caffeine was my drug of choice.

Now it's you.

Thank you for being here, for reading, for reviewing, and for always brightening my day with your words of support on the fb page. You rock my world, and without you, there really would be no reason to write these stories.

Thank you.

E x

MA gets all gooey and romantic

The other day MA and I were talking about the Giles 3 book and beyond. As you know Giles and Molly's stories inter link.

Anyway, part way through the conversation I happen to mention who might be getting together right towards the end of the season arc.

MA: OMG! (*in a genuine valley girl voice*) I'm so glad they're getting together.

Ellie: but you're not into the romantic kinda stuff.

MA: I know! But I'm really excited about these two. I'm *soooo* glad.

Ellie (frowning): really?

Now just to put this into context, this is the guy who told me absolutely NO. LOVE. TRIANGLES. (Apparently that kind of drama stresses him out).

This is also the guy who spent - what? - all of 300 words on the BA/Michael get together.

And now he's excited about a couple of my characters getting together? WTF?

And for those who are entrenched in the Jolly (Joel and Molly) vs Miles (Molly and Giles) shipping, it wasn't one of those conversations. It was about another couple... just so you know there is still much to happen there before things are resolved.

Oh the dramas.

<<MIKE EDIT: Wow, there is pulling back the curtain to allow others to see some of the blood, sweat and tears of the publishing world... And then there is pulling back the THAT'S THE DAMNED SHOWER CURTAIN YOU TOOL!

Heheheh... I said 'tool.'>>

Poker and Trading

I tell people that the reason I moved to Austin was for one particular poker game.

They don't believe me.

But actually it's not that far from the truth.

It's was a BIG deciding factor when I came here to cat sit my friend's kitties. Her friend met me to give me the keys to the apartment and show me round and she invited me to her weekly poker game.

Full disclosure: at this point I'd never played a game of poker in my entire life. (Nor have I played many games. Card games or otherwise. Screwed up childhood etc etc)

Anyway, I had a blast just sitting and watching. What struck me was just what an awesome group of people there were here. Everyone was super helpful and keen to explain things to me. (They said it was coz I was a girl... but I've always been a girl and never felt that included.) What also struck me was that there was a real sense of community.

And the more I watched, the more I could see that this was the sense of community I'd been looking for all the time I was feeling isolated in LA.

So fast forward several months and I still hadn't played a single game. And then the season started and my friend got me on the list for their tournaments. I think I've played in four now. It's going well. I'm starting to remember the hands, and I end up hanging on in there until about half the players have been knocked out.

I'm sure a big chunk of this is beginners luck but I'm learning a tonne every week. It's fun. And it's my dose of interacting with humanity each week. (It was a good decision moving to Austin.)

Anyway, what quickly became apparent is that poker is a life skill.

<<MIKE EDIT: OMG! Did you just now make it that learning POKER is up there with … Important stuff? I'm calling you out for elevating a card game to LIFE SKILL.>>

Applying to all kinds of things in business and life. I'm watching how my decision-making process on projects is shifting and being influenced by the way of thinking I've needed to adopt to take on the poker tournaments.

I'm also starting to understand the weird psychology underneath why people do certain things, like attach to pots, keep calling even with a losing hand, putting more into the pot than you can expect to get back (in terms of the expectation value… bad bets).

And I'm starting to see patterns in why people have moods and get stressed out – even if they're cool people away from the poker table. It seems that a lot of guys get angry and frustrated when they get knocked out. It's a strange phenomenon. I mean, the odds are that even if you're a decent player you're not going to win your money back. You only get a cash prize if you place in the top four. And it's not a lot of money either way.

And yet there seems to be a frustration when one doesn't win.

Plus, things tend to get tense at certain points in the game.

When blinds are about to go up at the end of a round.

When there are a certain number of people left before everything moves to one table.

When people lose chips(!)

I've noticed more than a few folks get funny and disappear straight after they get knocked out. It was a shock at first and it's taken me a few weeks to expect it when it happens.

If poker is a reflection of life, these are interesting data points.

Some of the guys have taken to teasing me when I get knocked out and get excited about where I placed in the rankings. Apparently I should be more moody and flip a table over or something. Ha! Never going to happen... but watching it all is helping me to understand humans a bit better.

My dentist is a closet geek

You may have seen on facebook that the crowning of the teeth continues. One of them has resulted in a root canal and been giving me no end of pain.

I've noticed a few folks in the comments making dental porn jokes, but I'm sorry to report there has been no dental porn here in Austin. This dentist is a little more earnest and doesn't have the same sense of humor as Dr. Mojito so I haven't mentioned it to him.

But when I asked to see my x-ray of a particular tooth he did get quite excited.

Then, the other day when he couldn't get me numb, he went and grabbed a text book to explain to me why (in theory!) I should be numb.

When I asked for some ibuprofen, when his fancy injections weren't working, he sent the nurse to grab some. She asked me for the dosage. I told her 400 mg. He was like: "hang on, who is the doctor around here?"

It was hilarious. And he had a point.

We talked about the memes that do the rounds on facebook:

Please do not confuse my medical degree with your google search.

He pulled out this one:

Patients will be charged extra for annoying doctor with their self-diagnosis found on the internet.

That was me.

He's also confessed to taking naps in his office at lunch time, but then talks about going out drinking with his friends all the time. I think that secretly he's a geek who lives a double life. His friends think he's a party animal. And at work he's just the boss. And then he has this really geeky quality that he seems to suppress.

Or maybe that's what my writer's mind is extrapolating.

Anyway. No dental porn conversation with this one.

But on the point of ibuprofen – I've ended up taking a boat load of pain killers for dental pain recently. I feel like I was just getting back on track and then this hit. I did a bit of reading about NSAID (Non-steroidal Anti-Inflammatory Drugs) the other day. (Not on the internet though!)

I knew ibuprofen is really bad for us but I wasn't sure exactly why. Turns out it attacks the intestinal track, amongst other things, causing lesions and leaky gut even. I wonder if this has been why I might be feeling sub-par.

I read up about some alternatives and order up some more supplements.

Turmeric.

I knew it was good for inflammation generally, but in a high enough dosage it can act as a pain killer.

It just arrived in the post while I was writing these notes. (Thank you Amazon!) Going to give it a try.

Fingers crossed.

<<MIKE EDIT: Seriously? Shit, I've been taking it for a while (not always every day) but certainly didn't think it was bad for us. *Dammit!* Now I have to worry.>>

Ellie vs the Red monkey

Writing is hard. It takes huge amounts of focus for long period of time.

To the outside world it looks like we're just sitting at a laptop all day. Vegetating.

The reality is very different.

And it's taken me a loooong time to really internalize this.

I've had writer friends who have explained that it can be as physically hard as running for hours. There's sciency stuff to support these claims.

Anyway, in an attempt to make it easier, lots of us use things like caffeine and adaptogens, just to keep going. (Caffeine is mostly off my list these days).

I've had a long interest in biohacking: how to increase human performance, physically and mentally. I've tried all kinds of supplements to this end, but for the most part have tried to get off anything that isn't natural and life supporting.

Yesterday was different though.

Yesterday was Saturday and between dental pain from a root canal on Monday and general exhaustion and lethargy I hadn't written anything all week.

As a writer who lives and dies by the word count this was BAD.

Instead, I'd been binging on Netflix and trying to recoup

enough to get some serious work done. I even ended up watching the series of *Limitless* for a bit of vicarious motivation.

Combine utter frustration with watching that show and of course certain things re-enter the mind. I remembered I have a cupboard full of biohacking stuff that I'd stopped taking. (Some of the side effects of these things include lights dancing in front of the eyes, and extreme exhaustion equivalent to jetlag spring to mind).

Anyway, as I said, yesterday I just needed to get SOME-THING done.

So I took something I'd bought called Red Monkey.

It certainly got my ass moving. I'd written over 8k words on the new Giles book by lunchtime.

However by the afternoon I was kinda burnt out again, so I ate some carbs and tried to chill. And watch some Netflix... That's when the lights started dancing, migraine style. Need-lesstosay, despite my desire to go for a run or walk, I was bed-bound for the rest of the day. I took TWO naps before I eventually surrendering and went to bed for good... only to wake up around 11am the next day.

The moral of this story – everything comes with a price. 8k words on the page may have cost me a few hundred brain cells.

And though I haven't thrown those pills away, I think I'm going to be sticking to my adaptogen laced "coffee" and XCT oil for the foreseeable future.

<<MIKE EDIT: Ellie could lose a few million brain cells and I'd still be woefully overpowered in a thinking contest with her.>>

Plates vs Bowls

I feel like since moving to Austin I'm gradually putting down roots.

Not permanent-never-going-to-move-again kinda roots. But I've been making more of an effort to make friends and go out and stuff. I must say, it's actually a tonne easier here than in a lot of places I've lived. Partly because southerners are so damn friendly. And partly because Austin is just an awesomely inclusive community. I'm loving it.

In the past few weeks I've even purchased things that one might need if one is staying more than a few months. Things like bathroom scales. A dehumidifier. Another set of glasses, and extra bar stools so that friends can sit at the island and play Cards Against Humanity when I get around to having them over for drinks.

(Granted, the stools are still in a box from when they were delivered. But they're there and ready).

I've even learned to use the dishwasher!

Yup.

You read that right.

I had one in the apartment in LA. And most places I was airbnb'ing before. But my calculations on how much effort it would take to figure it out, plus buying the right capsule things to put it in, plus loading and unloading... I just figured it was more efficient to wash them by hand.

But then the other day I was like: *Come on Ellie. You can adult. Figure this shit out.*

<<MIKE EDIT: "You can adult." BWAhahahahaha.... I think this is a fabulous term.>>

So I did. I remembered to add dishwasher tablets to the shopping list and a few days later I ended up stacking it up with dirty dishes that I'd left and not washed up... and figured out which buttons to press. (Turns out there's just one – the 'on' button – and I need to push it twice).

It was surprisingly easy.

So I've been a dishwasher convert for the last week!

But this brought me on to another self-revelation.

I'm definitely a bowl girl.

Given a choice… I'd faaaar rather eat from a bowl, than a plate.

Even to the extent that this morning I hadn't put the dishwasher on (because my noise cancelling headphones had needed charging and I can't bear the noise on the inside of my skull while I'm in the apartment) and so all the bowls were locked in the dishwasher.

Choice 1: lift one out and wash it.

Choice 2: use one of the 20 plates sitting in the cupboard.

And it was a difficult decision.

I opted for a plate… but man, I gotto tell you… not happy. The cauliflower doesn't taste the same, and things tend to move around too easily, even when you've got a knife.

(Sometimes I watch myself and I wonder: how have I managed to survive so long?)

Anyway, yeah. This is what I'm mulling as I'm sitting here eating and writing these author notes.

Yeah, I'm gonna live alone forever…

<<MIKE EDIT: Doubtful, but I CAN imagine someone making a TV show about you.>>

MA is kicking me out of Kurtherian

So call me paranoid but this is definitely thing.

<<MIKE EDIT: It is NOT a thing. It is me making sure my collaborators can fish (look it up.)>>

Ever since I started writing with MA, well two weeks after we published the first Molly book, MA has been trying to get me to go out on my own and publish.

Yep. Without him.

I've never understood it.

<<MIKE EDIT: See note above, I've only explained this a bajillion times.>>

It makes (a million times) more financial sense for him to have me write in his universe for... well, forever.

<<MIKE EDIT: I'm actually good with this, but I just feel guilty some times cause of all that money coming my way and no, I'm not changing the percentages, you are already coming out ahead.>>

And as a collaborator I'm probably the lowest maintenance there is. Certainly in terms of ROI and maintenance, I'm a pretty efficient bet.

So I always get suspicious when he harps on about how I need to publish my own universe. My own books.

He says it's because he wants to see me succeed on my own.

But I always wonder if he's just trying to get rid of me.

Like today.

We were talking about author notes and he said I needed to mention the new universe I'm building so that you know what's going on. Even if it's just a little bit of insight. It feels like he's trying to get rid of me. (Why would anyone want to get rid of me though?)

Anyway, in case he's planning on axing Molly and/or Giles... Here's the low-down on the Ellie'verse.

I'm midway through Book 1 of the new Bentley Jones series. This is tech-mag. So scifi but fringe science more than hard science. It's set in the future in another sector of space away from earth.

It's also funny as hell. (Well, it makes me laugh anyway... and since the cards against humanity escapade, I've realised I have a pretty dark sense of humour when let off the leash! Who'd have thought?)

I'm also working with a friend and collaborator, Rex, on another series, which is set a few hundred years earlier.

It's still sci fi-ish, but the protagonist is a chick who can touch things and "read" the object's past/ future. I'm loving reading it. In fact, I find it not only incredibly relaxing and entertaining to read, even though I worked on the beats with him, but I find myself hassling him for the next segment for entirely selfish reasons. Obviously I'm keen for you to get to read it, too. (We're going to start publishing as soon as we have a few episodes in the bag, so you wont be waiting around.) But when I hit him up for status updates… it's primarily motivated by my own desire to read it.

And as you know by now, I'm not a reader.

So I'm guessing/(hoping?) that you'll also find this series pretty special.

<<MIKE EDIT: See, was that so fucking hard? I bet you aren't worried about going out of Kurtherian Gambit, you are secretly scared of sharing your projects with your fans. YUP! That must be it!>>

I'm head down working on Giles 3 right now. Those mysterious talismans aren't going to find themselves. But they are going to explain exactly what's going on in the final Molly arc.

If you haven't already caught up with our rogue space archeologist, I recommend catching up with that story line pretty soon, as it's about to become super relevant to our girl Molly.

That is, as long as MA doesn't kick me out of Kurtherian…

<<MIKE EDIT: Nope.>>

E x

First, THANK YOU for not only reading our story, but reading our Author Notes as well. We can't do what we do, without you reading our work(s) and enjoying them.

<u>I Have a Confession!</u>

I really, REALLY didn't want to go down the Sean Royale getting married arc in these stories.

Ellie has been working on this for a while, and I had to trust her, but I didn't necessarily WANT us to go there.

Especially with this other character Katrina.

<<Ellie edit: you maybe should have mentioned this BEFORE we started this arc in the last book perhaps? (eyeroll) >>

<<<MIKE EDIT: I DID … perhaps I wasn't loud enough?>>>

I have to admit; I was wrong…. That's right, I typed it. (and I'm sure Ellie will mention this in the audio notes again… (Or stay very quiet like it isn't a big deal.))

<Small aside, are you listening to the audio books? We have quite a few out, check out our Molly books!>

So, I was in Texas during Spring Break with the two college guys coming back for a week (that was a strange experience all on its own.) I'm speaking with Ellie and there is an opportunity to read book 09 early so I ask for it.

I was messed up (sleepy) from the time zone and the whole allergy stuff. I started the book at night, enjoying myself but finally had to admit that sleep was going to win. I picked it back up the next morning right away, and then again a little later that morning when I was reading on the couch.

DAMMIT! Ellie had me. Actually, she had me back at the beginning and the whole arc with Sean was a fucking blast. I called her later that day to congratulate her on such a fun ride. I enjoyed the story, but hadn't finished it yet and had to admit that to her.

(I was working on a project that I got in over my head.)

So, now that I've finished the story I have (not the finished version). I will admit there are MANY laugh-out-loud moments.

But, the one that probably takes the cake for me was when Molly pulled Sean aside as he was standing at the front of the Church.

She is getting ready to blast him out of there, and he says he can't. He needs to take care of Katrina and if they leave, she is as good as dead.

So, Molly starts to reach for her gun, to (I assumed) cap one in Katrina's head to help her along.

Now, I may be a bit morbid, but I found that funny as hell. Molly is so focused on Sean, that she has NO issues capping his supposed bride in order to help him out.

Friends will lie for you. Good friends know where the bodies are buried. Molly is obviously a good friend!

<< Ellie Edit: OMG. I didn't think anyone would notice that! It was such a throw away line, and I figured most of y'all speed read so you know… It amused me when I wrote it too. >>

Wednesdays and Poker

So, Ellie and I have a standing conference call on Thursday's. It's like at 3:00 PM her time, 1:00 PM my time. (She is in Texas

(Austin), I'm in Las Vegas. Note how I stipulate the state before the city for her, and all I do is mention the city for me. I don't know how many people KNOW where Nevada is, but mention Las Vegas and they get it.)

Anyway, we are talking during our call, and we are going back and forth about a lot. Now, Ellie is NOT looking real spunky.

<<Ellie Edit: spunky in English means something else entirely! :-0 >>

In fact, she is looking rather less energetic than normal. Not that I'd let that change my opinion on if I could put one over on her. Even if she is running on four cylinders, she's still smart enough to carry on two conversations and chew gum.

<<Ellie Edit: I'd been up aaaaaaall night and was exhausted. >>
But, I digress.

So, we are chatting about stuff and she mentions 'blah blah blah, can't focus...' and I smirk. Why do I smirk?

Because I *know* what day of the week it is, and she has mentioned her new obsession that is both geeky, fun and involves statistics and people reading.

Our Favorite English Author™ loves *POKER*.

<<Ellie Edit: did you just trade mark me?>>

<<<Mike Edit: Yes, yes I did.>>>

So, this is our conversation over the Zoom line as I see her struggle trying to keep her eyes open. They keep glancing to the side (I'm assuming she needs caffeine.)

Me: Did you go to poker last night?

Ellie: (She perks up, like just mentioning the game and the party puts her into a new mindset.) YES!

Me: So, that explains why you are wiped out, stayed up late did we?

Ellie: (Eyes narrowing, realizing that I busted her.) *Yes...* (Then, she re-animates) Oh Oh! You had to see it, I got into the final hands, and some of the guys...

Ellie goes on to explain how some of the players react, and

whether or not she understands the emotions that they are going through when they have lost their pot. (Pots, I might add, she took from them.)

Oh, she understands the emotions intellectually, but whether she agrees on the efficacy of those feelings and allowing them to affect the person is a completely other discussion.

What is so compelling for me about her poker stories (and this is Ellie in a nutshell) is she didn't know ANYTHING about Poker before (or if she did, it was very little) and now after a handful of times playing, she is making it to the final game.

I would have been playing with the kids over in the corner, hoping the seven year old didn't call me on my pair of eights and high King!

I had a great five minutes as she recounts the stories from her poker night. Then, I ask her about her Cards Against Humanities night from a week or two back, and she laughs telling those stories.

I just want to say *"I Tried."*

I tried to get Ellie to record a Cards Against Humanities game with her author friends and put it up for all of us to listen, but she doesn't believe it will happen.

I'm rather bummed.

Stay with us as Molly has to do something she has been training for her entire life. She has to save her system from doing the unthinkable.

And it will take all of the intelligence, teamwork, family connections, spiritual understanding and guns (that's right, GUNS) to accomplish nothing less than...

Saving the world.

Ad Aeternitatem,

Michael Anderle

The Ascension Myth
*** With Michael Anderle ***

Awakened (01)
Activated (02)
Called (03)
Sanctioned (04)
Rebirth (05)
Retribution (06)
Cloaked (07)
Bourne (08)
Committed (09)
Subversion (10)
Invasion (11)
Ascension (12)

Confessions of a Space Anthropologist
*** With Michael Anderle ***

Giles Kurns: Rogue Operator (1)

<u>Giles Kurns: Rogue Instigator (2)</u>

The Second Dark Ages
with Michael Anderle
Darkest Before The Dawn (3)
Dawn Arrives (4)
Deuces Wild
with Michael Anderle
Beyond The Frontiers (1)
Rampage (2)
Labyrinth (3)
Birthright (4)

BOOKS BY MICHAEL ANDERLE

For a complete list of books by Michael Anderle, please visit:

www.lmbpn.com/ma-books/

All LMBPN Audiobooks are Available at Audible.com and iTunes. For a complete list of audiobooks visit:

www.lmbpn.com/audible

Receive updates from Oz by registering your holo/ email address here:
ellleighclarke.com

Facebook:
http://www.facebook.com/ellleighclarke/

Michael Anderle Social

Website:
http://kurtherianbooks.com/

Email List:
http://kurtherianbooks.com/email-list/

Facebook Here:
https://www.facebook.com/TheKurtherianGambitBooks/